RIVERS FOR STORMS

FROM THE MIND OF
TESHELLE COMBS

This story is currently available in serial format on the Kindle Vella platform.

Rivers For Storms can be read on its own, but to get maximum enjoyment out of the story, read Ripples For Skies before reading this book.

For the ones who learned to run.

RIVERS FOR STORMS WORLD TERMINOLOGY

Crylia (*cr-ill-yuh*) – the realm of the superior griffin race

Cryl/Crylia (*cr-ill*) – a griffin (part eagle, part lion, part serpent) who can take on a humanlike appearance, some notably devoid of usual human emotions and affections

Tru (*troo*) – a network of human villages collected into one tribe

Tru-ori (*troo-oh-ree*) – Tru humans with golden features

Tru-hana (*troo-ha-nah*) – Tru humans with blue features

Gua (*gwah*) – goddess of water, patron goddess of the Tru tribe

Miror (*mee-roar*) – the world

Cza (*zah*) – the indisputable ruler of the Crylia, also known simply as the King

Common Cryl – everyday language of Crylia

Old Cryl – ancient Cryl language, saved for incantations, Royal commands, or official purposes

Grounded – Cryl who have lost their wings, either by accident or as a form of punishment; lowest class

General – Cryl who lead armies on behalf of the Cza; First General is the highest rank

Teth – a male Cryl dedicated to the Cza at birth, tethering him in service all his life

Grand Teth – an elevated Teth

Teth-wed – a female Cryl married to a male who is tethered to the Cza

Black wings – the rarest of Cryl and the most severe and cunning

White wings – Cryl who are not as rare but very imperial and pretentious

Gold wings – Elevated Cryl and often rare and noble

Silver wings – Elevated Cryl who are often indifferent and intellectual

Gray wings – These Cryl are usually in the servant class and have more humanlike tendencies

Red wings – These Cryl are known for their impulsivity and cruelty

Zyesa (*zyes-suh*) - White wing Teth good at torturing for the Cza

Hresh (*resh*) - White wing Teth good at hunting bounty for the Cza

Krov vanya crystin - Pureblood Heir, literally translated 'Trail of Pure Blood' in Old Cryl

SOME NAMES IN RIVERS FOR STORMS

Emyri Izela (*em-er-EE, iz-AY-luh*) – Tru-ori spy, Nkita's partner

Nkita Opas (*nick-EE-tuh, OH-pass*) - black wing, Grand Teth, First General, Em's partner

Hrogar (*RO-gar*) – one-eyed gray wing rebel

Urol (*yoo-role*) – a gray wing tavernkeeper from Yogdn

Umra (*oom-ruh*) – a gray wing female, tavernkeeper's wife

Letti (*let-tee*) – you'll have to discover who she is

Cyndr (*sin-der*) – Crylia slaver and rebel

Drosya (*JRO-syuh*) – an old crylia female Grounded

Dagon (*DAG-uhn*) – red wing rogue and friend of Nkita

Yahara (*yah-ha-rah*) – Tru scout commander

Cevae (*sih-VAY*) – Tru scout and friend of Em

Mahopi (*mah-HO-pee*) – Tru scout and friend of Em

Miasi (mee-YAH-see) – Queen of the Tru

Kashila (*ka-SHEE-la*) - an old Tru woman from the town of Kiepo

1

The Day The General Caught The Spy

Gua teaches us that it is not we who hold the water, but the water who holds us. Yet the greatest miracle is not that the water holds us...it is that Gua teaches.

He will never forgive me for this.

But I didn't need Nkita to forgive me; I needed him to stay alive. The two of us together were more than a liability. We were a death sentence.

"Look up at me again, and I'll knock your teeth right out of your mouth, muckeater!" A burly Cryl hurled his apple core in my direction, spitting on the ground as I hurried past. His gray wings fullspread, he hissed until I was out of earshot.

Of course, he'd seen the metal ring in my lower lip. And of course, he despised me for it. But removing the ring could mean a worse fate. If I was found out to be a Grounded while failing to distinguish myself as such,

I'd be executed without trial and without mercy. And so I wore the ring, which gave these Cryl the right to say whatever they wished to me.

I pulled the hood of my cloak tighter over my head and bit my lip in, ducking behind a rolling carriage. If only I could get through town and into the woods. The perils among the trees would prove to be quite substantial, but at least it would be more difficult for Nkita to find me.

I picked up my pace, keeping my feet light, though I was more than tired, though the soles of my boots scraped along the packed dirt of the main road.

Things had been easier in the Capital of Crylia. Playing the part of a servant had taken its toll on me. It meant spending my days on my hands and knees, but there, I had friends. There, I had a cot to sleep in and an expectation of general decency when I walked the streets.

Outside of the Capital, Cryl with no wings—Grounded as we were called—were shown little respect. No, these woodland Cryl were vile and rageful even toward their own kind. In the Capital, the elites would expect me to avert my gaze, to hold my tongue in their presence. Those tethered to the Great Cza never really cared what I had to say anyway. But not so here. In the woodlands, a misplaced word could lead to talons around my throat.

Yet, Nkita and I could not go back to the Capital. Not ever. For there was a truth we needed to keep hidden. I was less than a servant, less than a Grounded.

An icy hand gripped my wrist and pulled me to an alleyway between two slumping buildings. When at last we were in the shadows, I yanked my arm away. If anyone had seen me so defiant in the street, I would have been arrested. But the shadows were my protection. The shadows...and the General.

"Where do you think you're going?"

I stared up into the face of the one questioning. Hair as black as the first darkness, skin like ivory, and lilac eyes boring into mine. I knew that beneath his cloak he had an onyx wing tucked behind his shoulder. Just the one. On his other side, he bore a scar deeper than the two I wore on my back.

"Do not drag me across town and then question me meaninglessly in an alley, Nkita," I snapped at him. The weather was cold enough for my breath to come out in clouds. I began looking about, making sure no one could see us speaking.

"I had few options, Emyri. I could not very well question you in the middle of the square, could I?"

"Do not question me at all!"

His voice was low and smooth, making my toes curl in my boots. I wanted him to whisper against my temple, to run his cold hands beneath my skirts.

"Well, what would you have me do with my questions, hm?" Nkita asked. "Because it certainly seems like you are running away from me. Again."

"Perhaps you should mind your own business, oh great General."

"I am not a General anymore, Emyri. And you are the only business I have left. What else should I be minding?"

"Perhaps I am finished with you. Ever consider that possibility? Maybe that's why I am leaving."

"If you were finished with me, you would have had a conversation. You would tell me exactly what I did that was so wrong, so evil, that now you've fallen out of love with me and never want to see me again. We both know I have done very, very wrong and evil things."

"Perhaps I am beyond explanations—"

"Emyri Izela, you are my *mate*."

"Shh!" I smacked Nkita's broad, perfect chest and felt my hand bones crunch out of place. *Gua help me, why is he built like this?* "Do not say such a thing out loud, Nkita! If these woodland Cryl knew that you and I were wed, that you are Teth and have married a Grounded—"

"I understand the stakes."

"Then you will let me run very far away from you, Nkita."

"Stop running from me, Em. It's ridiculous. I won't let anyone harm you."

If they find out I am worse than Grounded, there will be nothing you can do to stop them. "If they find out you are Teth and fleeing the Cza, Nkita, they will...they will send you back. And I can't let that—"

"Come. Home."

"I am going to get us caught. Unless you forgot—"

"I *know* what you are, Em," he growled. He wrapped a strong hand into my hair and tilted my head so I had no choice but to look right into those glittering eyes. "You're my mate. And we're going home."

But no. No, we're not going home. We're going to a hut that barely holds against the wind. And the only reason I was his mate was because we had no choice in the matter.

What I was...what I'd been would get us both killed. Not a winged-monster. Not a flightless Grounded. But a human spy deployed to destroy the Crylia.

A human. A Tru.

A weakness.

2

THE DAY THE GUARDIAN PLOTTED

"I see you brought her home," Hrogar said. He carried a deer over his shoulder, glaring at me through his good eye. "And I hope you taught her a lesson for running off."

I narrowed my gaze at the stocky Crylia male, balancing my bundle of fresh-chopped wood in my arms. He wouldn't be finished with his blabbering. Not yet.

"I'm telling you, General," Hrogar continued, "a high-spirited female like that? She needs a good thrashing to be kept in line. And you're just the Cryl to do it."

I stood watching him as he spoke, my mouth shut, though not out of habit. He dropped the deer on the ground, pine needles and mud flying as it landed. "You just lay her out over your knees and let her have it," he explained. "And when she's finished, she can busy herself with skinning this meat—"

That was enough for Nkita. He left the doorway, where he'd been repairing the shoddy hinges, walked over to Hrogar Gray Wing, and shoved him backward so that he fell hard on his arse. Then, he made his way to me and took the bundle of wood from me. He tucked it under one of his arms and wrapped the other arm around my waist. He lifted me over to the cracked wooden deck of the house we shared with Hrogar.

"Go do whatever you'd like," he said.

I cleared my throat, trying to pretend I was not blushing at the sentiment. "And if what I like is chopping wood?"

"Well, I suppose that's too bad for the wood."

"Oh? You'll not be putting me over your knee, then?"

His lilac eyes bored into mine. "When I'm ready."

Cryl be damned. When he's ready? I headed inside before he could see how deeply my golden skin flushed. I was fortunate I'd been born a Tru-ori. Humans from my tribe either bore blue markings or gold ones. Gold meant I could disguise myself as a gold wing among the Crylia monsters. If I had been born Tru-hana, I would have been groomed for a life of warmongering instead.

But it had not always been that way. We were not always spies and soldiers. The Tru once were people of the water. Gentle and humble and honest. *What would the goddess think of us now?* I shook my head, banishing my thoughts. It didn't matter what Gua would think. Not if we failed to survive our systematic annihilation at the hands of the winged Crylia.

Hrogar entered the house, shaking mud off his boots and growling at me. "How a Teth like Nkita ended up

13

with a Grounded like you is beyond me," he said. "I mean you no harm, Grounded. I just don't understand it."

How Nkita ended up with me? Perhaps I should just tell the grumpy Cryl. He had been assigned by the rebels to keep us safe, after all. *Perhaps I should just tell him that Nkita caught me spying for the Tru and fell in love with me. Perhaps I should just tell him that the Great Cza used me to bend Nkita to his will, nearly killing him in the process. Perhaps I should tell him that Nkita gave up his entire life—his standing as a Teth, his occupation as a General, his honor as a Cryl—to run away with me. To keep* me *safe.*

Perhaps I should just tell him that he was right. I would be the undoing of the black wing Cryl who called me his mate.

"Mind your business, Hrogar," I said. "You speak of things you don't know."

"You're right," he said. "I don't know. I was ordered to hide the General from the Cza. And that was going to be hard enough. But now I have to hide his knobholder as well."

"If you hate having me here so much, Hrogar, you could help me escape instead of telling Nkita I've run every time."

Hrogar scoffed. "If I don't tell him you've run off, he will spend the rest of his life looking for you. And you won't be found. You'll be dead in the shack of some red wing who thought you looked pretty and took you for his plaything."

"And then your rebel mission will be derailed?"

"Exactly. Now you have some brains between those wings."

"I don't have any wings at all, Hrogar."

"Wouldn't be much of a problem if you did. Wouldn't even need the brains. You'd be an *acceptable* gold wing, and no one would take notice of the two of you together." He sat down on one of our shaky chairs and smacked his boots onto the table that was meant for eating. "At least you got creative this time. Cutting through the town. Took him a minute to realize you'd gone a different way."

I should try leaving at some other time of day. Maybe the dead of night. If I can get far enough, fast enough. Maybe keep to the rivers—

"I see you over there plotting and planning, Grounded."

"Leave me alone, Hrogar. Don't you have a deer to skin?"

"That's a female's work."

"You wouldn't catch a Teth-wed doing something like that in the Capital." Images of jewel-encrusted females with white wings and sparkling Crylia eyes filled my mind. I had left some of those beautiful females behind when I ran from the Capital. And none of them, not even servants like Nolyen, would be found skinning anything.

Hrogar spit on the floor and dragged the back of his hand across his scruffy, bearded mouth. "There aren't any fancy Teth-wed females here, Little Talon. Just gray wings with work on their minds and red wings with madness in their heads." He paused. "And you."

"The worst of the worst." All because he thought I'd lost my wings. But if he really knew that the scars on my back were given to me by my own people...that I was the enemy of all Cryl...he wouldn't think I was the worst of the worst. He would act on it.

"Worse than the worst of the worst," Hrogar clarified. "Because that gorgeous Crylia is all we rebels have left to hope in. But you're going to get him killed."

I sighed, throwing my hands in the air. "I know that, Hrogar. I *had* to marry Nkita! There wasn't an option. The Cza made sure we had no way out of our union, and now I'm here. What am I supposed to do? Die?"

Hrogar grew very serious, his scarred face still, his brown gaze steady, even if only one of his eyes peered at me. "We could have it arranged."

My blood grew chilled, every vessel and every vein freezing over. "You...seem serious."

"I am." He crossed hardened arms. "I could do it in your sleep—"

I jumped as Nkita walked in, carrying the deer Hrogar had left in the mud. "You," he said. "Go and finish your work out back."

"Out back?" Hrogar shivered. "But the cold is setting in. And I'm too old to keep up with these storms."

Ha! The cold is always setting in when it comes to Crylia climate.

"Get out," Nkita growled, shoving the deer into Hrogar's lap. And then, he turned to me. "And you? Come here."

3

THE DAY THE SPY RAN

I swallowed, wishing to Gua I wasn't blushing so fiercely. *Spies ought to be able to hide things better than this.* "I thought you were stacking wood."

"Finished with that."

"Oh." I looked at him. *Cryl be damned, he is just staring.* "Perhaps a rest is in order? I can go help Hrogar with the deer—"

Nkita crossed the room and put his hand on my waist. He gripped hard enough for me to feel the grooves of his fingers through my linen dress.

"You deserve more than this," he said, his voice low. "If I had my way, I would keep you in fine silk." He pulled me closer to him and, with his other hand, traced along my collarbone. "Fine jewels on your neck."

"We can't go back, Nkita," I told him. "We can never go back there."

"So why do you keep running off? Are you unhappy with me, Em?"

I had to clear my throat twice for words to come out, in part because I wanted to speak carefully, and in part because Nkita tightened his grip on my waist and slid his hand around to my back. "I am not unhappy with you, General."

When I looked down to evade his eyes, he lifted my chin. "I'm serious, Em. Tell me."

"I know. You're always serious. But I am not worried about you. It's the...the Cza."

"The King is not here, Em."

"He is coming. Coming for you. And if he can't take you down, he will take me in, Nkita. And you will yield to him, I know you will. I've seen you do it once. I can't watch you do it again."

I closed my eyes against the memory of the cold-hearted King ripping the wing out of Nkita's shoulder. Of blood pooling down the General's back as he endured it. All so the Cza would not harm me. Because although Nkita was Teth, tethered to the Cza since his birth, he was my mate. He would trade his very life for my safety. He would sacrifice every comfort for my happiness.

He didn't mind having me as a weakness. But I refused to be his downfall.

"You must know I will not apologize for doing what it took to keep you safe."

"I don't want an apology, Nkita. I want you to tell me you won't do it again."

There were few safe places for Tru like me in Miror. Few places to hide, few places where the Crylia would not find us, would not use their talons to rip us limb from limb. The war between our kinds had been raging for centuries, and fear was part of who we humans were.

I thought I was well acquainted with terror. Spying for my people had taught me that fear was necessary for survival. But never before had I felt fear like this. The true, humbling, heart-imprisoning fear of watching someone I loved being tortured to death on my behalf.

But Nkita held me to him, his chest against mine until my breath caught. "I am not going to stop wanting you. I don't care what it costs me."

I knew he wanted me right then. I could feel his heart slow in his chest, his intention narrowing in on me, on my body, on my every sensation. I still hadn't grown accustomed to the fact that he could *feel* me. Feel inside me with his very being. He knew I was breathless. He knew my fingers burned to touch him, that my skin prickled with the hope of his lips grazing mine.

"Let me," he whispered against my ear. "*Em.*"

I dug my nails into my palm and used the shot of pain as a distraction, pulling myself away from my mate. "I'm not ready."

Nkita scoffed. "Liar."

"You think you can feel what I feel, Nkita, but you don't know my thoughts. My reservations."

"I know enough to be confident that you are picking a fight with me on purpose right now."

I scoffed. "We *love* fighting."

"Is that why you're about to walk away instead of finishing our fight?" He held me like I belonged with him. "Stay put. Finish the fight."

"You're acting like a child."

"I have never even met a child. Aim your insults with a bit more precision would you."

"Fine! You are acting like an unhatched Crylia offspring. Better?"

"No. You think I'm acting like an *egg* right now? That's the best you can do? Em, you are not angry with me. Stop pretending."

"I am becoming angry with you. That is the whole point of picking a fight!"

"Well, I am becoming angry with you, and it only makes me want to take your clothes off more. So why don't we just *do that*?!"

"Because I have thoughts and...and *reservations*!"

"You wouldn't have either of those things if we just took your clothes off. That is my point!"

"Just because you married me doesn't mean you get to have me whenever it pleases you."

Nkita kept his place in the small room, the wind howling against the logs that held our new home together.

"I know that. Because it pleases me to have you every moment of every day, yet I haven't since we were wed."

"I don't want to talk about our wedding day."

Nkita closed his eyes and then, without another word, he left through the front door.

With him gone, I slumped into one of the chairs and let my face fall to my hands. *How long am I going to pretend I don't want this Cryl?* I shoved my golden hair back from my face and stood back up. "As long as it takes," I said to myself.

"My thoughts exactly."

I swiveled with a gasp. "Nkita! I thought you went outside."

"You were wrong. Here I am." He leaned against the doorframe. His onyx hair was growing longer every day, the muscles of his shoulder, neck, and jaw just as sharp as always, if not more so.

"Well, go away. I am brooding."

Nkita's eyes widened. "You...are brooding? Now?" Nkita stepped backward. "So...so soon?"

"What are you talking about?"

"Like...eggs?"

"What?! No, Nkita, not that kind of brooding. I am not a *hen*. I'm a woman."

"That's what we call it, Emyri. I thought you meant—"

"No, no, no. I am not...we haven't—" I sighed, trying to relax my shoulders. "My life isn't that far over yet, Nkita."

Hrogar called from the yard. "When do I get to come inside? This butchering is taking forever, and I can only warm myself for so long."

"Mind your deer, or I will shove you inside it and leave you for the bears," Nkita snapped. "I am still talking with my mate." Nkita slammed the door, stepping inside once more. "I hate him."

I grinned. "Me too. He's like if Old Zloy grew a fat beard."

A smirk tugged at the corner of Nkita's mouth. "You miss the groundskeeper?"

"Oh yes. Every morning I wake up and wonder, 'who will beat my knuckles, today?'"

"Well, if this gray wing ever lays a hand on you, I'll rip his head from his shoulders."

I licked the ring on my lip. "I know, Nkita."

"Seems like you don't."

Hrogar burst into the cabin, his arms drenched in blood up to the elbows, his sword drawn.

Nkita stepped between him and me, drawing his own sword, his only remaining wing spread as he prepared for the kill.

But Hrogar was not about to attack. "They found us," he said, breathless, eyes stern. "The Cza's guard is moving up the mountain."

Nkita wasted no time. "How many, how long?"

"Looks like twenty. I'd give us two minutes if we're lucky."

"We run," Nkita said. "Em, now."

But I was already moving through the back door, my feet quick as I plodded through the mud, arms pumping. I would be slower than the Crylia by far. I would take as much of a head start as I could get. It took me three whole minutes of darting through cypress trees to realize I had been fooled.

Nkita had stayed behind to hold them off.

Sacrificing himself for me. Yet again.

I'm going to kill him.

But then, I realized...he was occupied. And I was already on my way. My determination set in, and I took a deep, steadying breath. *Gua help the helpless. I am going to miss that Cryl.*

4

THE DAY THE WHITE WINGS CAME

The last thing Nkita would expect was for me to stay in the woodlands. In fact, he would be quite furious if he knew I'd chosen the crowded town of Yogdn to hide me. It was more dangerous for a Grounded in these parts of Crylia, and females were not safe either. The risks loomed before me, but my goal was not to avoid risk. It was to avoid my mate.

To get to Yogdn, I doubled back toward the Capital, hoping not to cross paths with the guards who were hunting for us. Then, I found the most meaningless employment I could attain.

"Ten pies of steamed cod," Urol shouted, though he was six inches from my ear. "Ten! No less, no more!"

I nodded, scooping a mound of flour into the big wooden bowl before me. More crust, more cod, faster. Faster. But the chance for quickness and pies was gone in an instant. Urol put his thick hand on me, gripping

25

me by the back of the dress and dragging me away from the counter where I worked.

"Go out there and pour the ale," he said.

I gulped. "Out there?" I peeked beyond the counter that kept my workstation separate from the rowdy tavern customers. "I—"

"I didn't ask if you preferred it, Grounded. You'll go."

Urol shoved a pitcher of ale into my chest, turned me around, and shoved me through the swinging kitchen door.

I stumbled forward, nearly spilling the contents of the warm pitcher. The Cryl males nearest me took interest immediately, their sharp eyes turned to me, soaking in the sight of me, making judgments on my status as well as on the curves of my hips and the swell of my breasts. They were a bit too full for a Crylia female. The lingering gazes of the males made me nervous for a myriad of reasons.

I began pouring for the first table, careful not to let my nerves show, keeping my hands steady. Gray wings sneered and spat on my boots as I filled their cups and bowls. Gray wings were the most like humans, and at least I could predict what their hatred felt like.

But there was a table of white wings in the corner of the tavern that gave me great concern. White wings were more pretentious, more intellectual in their hatred of others. They would *think*. Think about why a gold wing Grounded was in a Yogdn tavern sloshing out ale with trembling hands. And if they were from the Capital, they would know that Grand Teth Nkita Opas had married such a thing as a gold wing Grounded and that the two traitors were on the run.

Gua. What do I do?

"Fill my cup before I tell Urol he hired a sluggish one!" a gray wing shouted from across the tavern. I hurried to his table and began to pour. I kept my eyes on the white wings. But also...I listened. Because that's what spies do. They listen.

"Those white wings think they're something special, taking up room in our place," the gray wing said as I filled his cup, his large jowls shaking. "What business could they have in Yogdn?"

"Out looking for someone," another male said. "Something to do with the Cza's orders."

My blood chilled in my veins. *The Cza? Not good. Not good at all.*

"No," another Cryl chimed in, leaning in to share his version of the news. "It's not that. I heard they were off looking for that one wing General who carries the Cza's blood."

"Ha!" the fat one laughed. "You believe that story? Like the Cza would ever let a krov vanya crystin live past infancy, much less grow into a full-powered black wing General. I'll believe it when I see it!"

You'll not be seeing it. Not ever. Not if I have anything to do with it.

"So what're they here for, then? Eh?"

He leaned in even further. "Looking for
a Tonguekeeper."

The other two Cryl grew quiet.

The third shrugged. "It's what I heard."

"Go back to drinking your ale and shutting your mouth,
you blabbering common wing, before you mess with
things none of us understand," the fat one snarled. Then,
he turned on me. "You plan on lingering, Grounded,
or you going to do your job and fill our bellies?"

I gave a little bow and moved to the next table. All the
chatter was the same. Musings and speculations about
the white wings and why they were in Yogdn. But no more
mention of a Tonguekeeper, whatever that was.

A few tables later, after a refill of my pitcher, I ran
into a gray wing who had already had too much ale.
Instead of letting me pour, he grabbed hold of my arm
and yanked me forward. My thighs collided with the
rough wooden table, but I resisted him, twisting my arm
away. I would bear bruises by the morning, but they
would be indistinguishable from the black and purple
circles already plaguing my poor body.

No matter the resistance, the Cryl grabbed hold of my
skirts, belched and sneered, pulling me hard so I spilled
my ale and fell against his sweaty body.

"Stop," I told him firmly. "Enough."

"I will tell you when I've had enough, Grounded. And
it'll be when my ale is spilling out of you and not a
moment sooner."

I shoved myself off him while his comrades laughed at his advances. It wasn't until Urol huffed over and wrapped talons around my arm that I was disentangled from the drunken Cryl.

"No fair, Urol! Share!"

The tavernkeeper held a finger up to the sloppy monster, his other hand still squeezing the blood from my arm. "You can't even afford the ale sliding down your gullet, much less a night with my worker."

Urol dragged me back into the kitchen and threw me into the baking table, his gray wings fullspread behind him. He drove a strong backhand into my cheek, making me slice my lip with my teeth. I gurgled as my own blood slipped down my throat. He was about to strike me again when the room shifted.

"Have you eaten your dinner, Urol?" a female voice said.

Urol lowered his hand, his wild brows still arched in anger. But he turned to face the female Cryl. "Umra...."

"You know how you get when you haven't eaten," she said. She put a fist on her narrow hips—all Cryl females were narrow since they needed to fly and lay their speckled eggs, not to birth large babies like we Tru—and gave her mate a look. "Now, come on. Leave the Grounded be and come upstairs. Your food is getting cold."

"But...the muckeater spilled a pitcher of my ale—"

"And I am telling you to come upstairs"—Umra tilted her head toward him and gave him a look—"and get your dinner."

Urol smiled, revealing an array of missing teeth. "Oh. My dinner. I suppose I am a bit hungry."

"I thought you might be," Umra said. She led the way, leaving her greasy apron on the steps as her mate followed her.

I owed Umra for interrupting my immediate demise on more than one occasion. She had a soft spot for me, though only Gua knew why. And I would have thanked her by cleaning the kitchen extra well if it weren't for the three white wings silently standing amid the spilled barley and the cod pie crumbs. Staring straight at me.

5

The Day The Spy Escaped

I bowed my head, holding my tongue before the white wings. They would not take kindly to a Grounded speaking out of turn. The wingless were also to be the wordless.

One of the three white wings stepped forward, careful to step over the many puddles on the tavern kitchen floor. "Greetings, Grounded," he said. His sharp nose and keen eyes failed to soften his approach, though his words were peaceable enough. "We are looking for someone."

I fought the urge to back away. Doing so would only bring forth the predatory instincts of the winged monsters. They would corner me. I would be seen as prey. *Instead, I need to be boring. I need to be useful but not interesting, helpful but not desirable.*

"How may I aid you in your search?" I whispered. *Tell him what you will be doing. Assign your own tasks, or you'll be given one you don't wish for.*

"We need the present location of the tavernkeeper."

Urol? What do they want with him? I decided to play stupid. "I-is the food not to your liking?"

"We would never permit this gruel to sully our tongues."

I folded my hands before me, head still downcast. My hair—a tangled mess of dulling gold—falling over my shoulders. "What do you need from my employer, sirs?" I was hoping they would correct me, asking me to address them as Teth. Or Grand Teth. I wished to know if they were tethered to the Cza and doing his bidding. But they did not ask me to call them such.

"No more questions. Take us to him." The white wing leader took another step forward.

"I am not sure where he is. I will find him for you."

The white wing was close enough to strike me, his breath cool on my face as he looked me over. His scarlet eyes flicked about as he observed me. "A shame to have a lovely gold wing as a Grounded. Who took your wings, female?"

I pretended it was difficult for me to speak of it. "Humans attacked my village when I was young. Took the wings of all the helpless. Killed the rest." It was a lie, of course. I was a woman, born of a woman, like every woman before me.

"How hateful." The white wing reached out with manicured hands, touching my cheek as he studied my reaction. His voice was as cold as his hands. "But do not worry, you pathetic creature. We will end the convolution that is human beings once and for all. Now, fetch your master for us."

If Nkita knew how this Cryl spoke to me, how he put his hands on me.... But Nkita would never know. That was the point of me leaving him.

My brain burned as I turned away from the white wings. If I still had my connections to the Tru, I would tell them immediately what I had heard. But it would be much more useful information if I knew how these Crylia intended to destroy humans for good. I hurried up the stairs, bracing myself for what I would face.

Sure enough the sound of my decrepit employer ravaging his mate assaulted my ears. He grunted and groaned, while Umra remained perfectly silent, as a good Cryl female ought. *I will have to interrupt them. He will be furious. Also this is utterly disgusting.*

I knocked on their door, glancing up at the thatched ceiling above us. In more wealthy Crylia towns and cities, the ceilings were removable. During warmer weather, the Crylia could flit in and out of the houses without bothering to use doors. But in poor towns like Yogdn, the roofs stayed put. *At least the white wings cannot fly into the room.*

"Master Urol?" I asked, raising my voice to be heard over his wheezing and moaning. "Master Urol!"

The rocking did not end.

Cryl be damned, I will have to open this door. I twisted the handle, trying to hold myself together once I realized how sticky it was. Then I cracked the door open. "Master Urol. I hate to interrupt—"

There was no stopping the Cryl. So I opened the door all the way.

"There are three white wings downstairs who are looking for—"

Umra heard me. She shoved her husband off her in one move and swung her legs off the bed. "Death to the dying," she cursed, gathering a satchel form beneath her bed while her mate flopped onto the ground.

"You cursed female!" he shouted from the wooden planks. "What have you done? You could have broken my member!"

But Umra wasn't listening. She pulled her skirts back down over her legs and scrambled toward the window.

"Wait!" I cried out. "Umra...wait!"

"No time," she said.

"I know what they want. The white wings."

She smirked at me. "So do I."

"I can give you more information if you take me with you."

"You'll slow me down. And I don't need more information. I need to *live*. You really think they want this fool? They only think they want him because I am *clever*."

"They'll...they'll force me if you leave me." I took a deep breath and made my plea. "I will owe you my life if you take me with you. Umra. Please."

She sighed. "I suppose I can make a slave useful. Come on, before this loud fool lets them know I'm fleeing."

"You can't fly away from me," Urol shouted, finally righting himself. "I demand you lie back down—"

But I crossed the room wrapped my arms around Umra's neck. She leaped from the window and took to the air, surprisingly strong arms around my middle. "Pomo jyo, sya sya," she said. And with that, my eyes closed, and the darkness of the night became all I knew.

6

THE DAY THE NAME WAS REQUESTED

"Rare to find a gold wing in these parts. That's the first of your mistakes."

I awoke with my cheek pressed to the fallen twigs and crushed leaves of the forest floor. With a gasp, I pulled myself up and took in my surroundings. No one was near. No one but Umra.

The Crylia female hung bits of clothes on tree branches. The cloth dripped onto the sod below, and a sudden rush of longing overtook me. It was so rare for me to wish I were home. To miss the sounds of rushing rapids and the slow trickle of winding creeks. To feel Gua's presence strong and fierce as water poured from the clouds. We Tru had never longed to take to the skies like the Crylia monsters. It wasn't our place to enter Gua's domain, to climb into the heavens on our own wings. We liked our place on the ground. And we were grateful she sent water down to meet us, to heal us, to love us.

"Gold wings and white wings keep to the bigger cities," Umra carried on. "Where the food is rich and the company *snobbish*. You? Out here all alone? Shoveling shite pies and pouring stale brew in a shady tavern? It's suspicious. Makes it real clear you're hiding something. Or hiding *from* something." Umra clicked her tongue as she wrung out the skirt she'd been wearing earlier. Her wings spread wide, drying in the cool morning air. "That, and you're too smart. Far too smart. You like to play dumb, but we both know you should have had your behind taken half a dozen times by now, and you've evaded every single attempt from every single male."

"Thanks to your help," I said, my voice raspy from sleep.

"No. You'd have figured it without me. Would have been harder, but you'd have managed. Didn't you manage before me, Grounded?"

"I suppose."

"You either managed to not be taken or you didn't. Which was it?"

"Didn't."

"Well, there you go. Too smart."

"It's suspicious that I am able to keep myself safe?"

"It is. You should be an idiot."

"I've not met a stupid Cryl female in all my days." My words were sharper than I should have allowed them to be. I cleared my throat. But she'd angered me. I'd met females, like Mlika White Wing, who were both kind and clever. My dear Nolyen, who was as noble and humorous a gray wing as any Cryl could be. A servant named Rhaza who'd shoved Nkita and me out of a window, saving our lives when the Cza sought to take us to our graves. But that was not what Umra needed to hear. So I changed my approach. "I...don't mean to disrespect you, Umra. I am a bit confused about where I am. I've been trying to remember what I am doing here—"

The much older Crylia turned on me, her finger pointed. "See? That. That right there. You have a sharp tongue, but you pretend you don't. I am not inquiring as to why you speak your mind, Grounded. I am asking why you have a mind to speak."

I need to change this subject. "I could ask you the same thing, couldn't I? Why were those white wings looking for your mate? And why did you think that meant they were really looking for you?"

She scoffed, returning to her wash. She had changed into a dress, no doubt from the satchel she'd kept packed under the bed above the tavern. *That means she knew this could happen.* She'd been prepared to run at any moment. "I said I would make you useful, not tell you my business. Besides, we're both better off apart from that wormsucker."

"He'll be looking for you, though. Won't he? Urol is your mate after all."

"I'll sever our ties. He'll feel nothing for me."

I hid my shock, standing and stretching sore limbs. I had many, many questions for this Umra, this tavernkeeper's mate. *How did she put me to sleep so fast? How did she fly without me weighing her down? Why was she prepared to flee? And...how in the name of Gua would she be able to sever the bonds between Cryl and mate?*

But I needed to ask the right ones. If I put her on edge, I would get no answers at all.

"Where are we now, Umra?"

"Far."

Far. That means far from Nkita. Far from Hrogar and the muddy little cabin. But what have we gotten close to? "Are we nearer to the Capital, then?"

"Past it."

A shot of panic, starting from the soles of my feet and flooding up to my chest. No wonder I missed the water of my people. If we'd crossed over the Capital, it meant we were nearing the borders of Crylia. It meant we were nearing Tru. Returning to my people would mean a fate worse than returning to the Cza, that much I knew.

"I know what you're thinking. Don't worry so much, Grounded. I won't let the humans near you"—Umra put her hand on her hip. She shoved gray, coarse hair away from her face. "What even is your name?"

When Nkita met me, I was Syiva. When my people loved me, I was Emyri Izela.

But who will I be to this stranger? What lie will my life tell now?

"I am Oahra."

"Call me Letti."

"Pleased to meet you." I bowed. *A spy knows when she's in the presence of her own.*

"Now, tell me the name of the mate you're fleeing from, and I will sever his bond with you as well." She crossed her arms. "With haste. From the measures you've taken to hide from him, I can tell we don't want him showing up to claim you."

I stared, wordless.

"Oahra. The *name.*"

7

The Day The Mountains Cursed

The truth doesn't care much for kindness. It doesn't belabor its own revelations. So I stood in the cool morning sun and confessed to myself that I could not bear to be severed from the Cryl I loved. I closed my eyes for a moment and imagined the pain—and the unbridled rage—he would feel if I was no longer his mate. And I couldn't do it.

But could I tell this Leiti the truth? That the reason I wasn't at Nkita's side was because I loved him with every bit of my soul?

Of course I cannot. She could be anyone. She could want anything. I could be risky with myself, but not with him.

"I will leave the severing to you, Letti."

But she didn't buy it. "You will give me the name, or I will leave you where you stand. I'll not be bringing a target along with me."

"Where are we going?" I hoped to distract her.

She stared at me, her eyes narrowed. She was not like any Crylia female I had ever met. Not as crafty as Mlika, perhaps, but just as clever.

I decided to use my information. That was its purpose anyhow. To be used. "Tonguekeeper, they call you?"

Letti began removing her still-wet clothing from the branches and stuffing them back into her satchel.

"Letti, tell me why you're running from white wings looking for a Tonguekeeper." *Maybe I can figure out what that is.*

"I was wrong," she said. "You are completely useless."

"I am trying to help—"

"Then give me the name of your mate and shut up about things you don't understand."

I can't let her leave me here. Not so close to the Tru border. Spying for my people had been following orders. But if they thought I was crossing the border...if the Tru thought I was trying to get home—I took a quick breath and steadied my nerves. "Forgive me for speaking out of turn. My mate's name...is Rizel."

Letti paused, her cheeks going pale.

"Do you...know him?" I asked. *Oh no. What if this Umra-turned-Letti had lived in the Capital, eating and drinking with Rizel at Vecherins. She might catch me in my lie before I've even begun to tell it.*

"No, I don't know any Rizel," she replied. "But I have heard of him. And if indeed you are tied to a Cryl that powerful, we will need more than this to sever your bond."

"More than...what?"

"More than words, Grounded." She nodded her head toward the sunrise. "We go east. To the mountains."

"To *which* mountains?" *Please don't say Led. Please don't say Led.*

"Led is where we need to be. And with haste."

Oh no. Now I have gone and made everything worse. Led is where exiles are sent when the Cza is finished with them. "Perhaps, perhaps I should not slow you down. You can go on without me, Letti. I will make due."

"You will come," she said. "You said you owe me your life. And so you will."

"But—"

"I have need of you." Then she wrinkled her nose. "But there is time for you to bathe first. A river is near here."

"I can hear it rushing." *And I can feel it calling to me.* But that part was best to keep to myself.

"Bathe."

"Letti...how did you carry me here? You are not any larger or stronger than me—"

"Bathe."

I left the Crylia and followed the sound of the river, the water calling to me. The bottoms of my feet tingled in my boots until I was compelled to remove my footwear and place my toes in the crystal flow. I sighed. "Gua sends her rivers through the barren lands," I whispered, barely moving my lips, though no one was present. "As the water flows between them, she gives even the stones a purpose."

I plunged into the deep flow, holding my breath as the water kissed my filthy skin. When I surfaced—after far too long, since Cryl did not usually enjoy getting their wings wet—I thought I saw a blur of motion in the trees. But I stared until my eyes crossed and saw nothing more but insects coming to life and leaves rustling in the breeze. I left the water behind me and began my walk back to Letti.

"Better to have you sopping wet than to have you smelling like Urol's pies."

"I am glad to be rid of his stench as well."

Letti frowned at me. "Do you know how many bruises you bear, Oahra?"

I glanced down at my chest, my arms. The fabric of my feeble dress clung to my thinning body. "Many?"

"You look like I enjoy beating you. We shall have to find you a coat to cover all this up. Not every Cryl takes well to masters who beat their slaves."

I nodded. "If it suits you." *Thank Gua.* I could not regulate my temperature as Cryl could. Without a coat, the mountains of Led would freeze me to death on the first night.

"Lie down and go to sleep," Letti said. "Close your eyes."

"Sleep? But I have only just awakened for the day—"

"Do as you're told."

I curled myself up on the ground, bewildered at her request. "Pomo jyo, wyo wyo," she whispered.

Sleep took me in an instant, and I awoke completely dry and nestled in a warm fur coat, snow and icy wind ripping through my hair. I nearly screamed when I realized I had been asleep on the very edge of a cliff, surrounded by nothing but white.

"The ground is playing tricks on us," Letti called. I looked this way and that and finally found her a ways below me, her gray wings fullspread. "No matter. This works just fine."

I stood, staring down at her, careful not to slip and fall to my doom. The snow-capped crags of the Led Mountains loomed above me. If I squinted, I swore I could see the frozen bodies of the Cryl the Cza had exiled, monsters who'd died alone and without hope because they could not please their king.

"Letti, would you come and get me down?" I asked. Already the cold soaked through my bones.

"I am sorry," she said, her lips pulled into a frown. "But I need to survive this."

Em, do not lose your composure now. Do not let fear overtake you. But my heart pounded in my chest anyhow. "Survive...what? Letti...survive what?"

"Forgive me, but I will have to make you useful after all."

The sound of wings flurrying, that haunting and familiar sensation of wind beating against my bones.

I refused to turn around. In truth, I was too afraid. "What...did you *do*, Letti?"

"When you said his name, I knew he would be looking for you. He...can get me what I need, Oahra. I had to."

His voice scratched down the back of my neck. Only once in my life had I heard it. And once was enough. "Why if it isn't the Grounded who took my very life from me." Rizel. The black wing General. "Won't this be fun?"

8

THE DAY THE BLADE TURNED

Rizel waited until Letti approached him before tossing her a small cloth sack. "If I ever see you again, it will be at your own misfortune," he warned the gray wing.

She looked at me one last time before she took flight over the icy gorge beneath.

All that was left for me to do was to face Rizel. I knew not what he wanted with me or why he would make a trade for me at all, but I knew one thing for certain. Whatever Rizel had planned for me...it was a worse fate than I would have faced at the hands of those white wings in Urol's tavern.

And so, while there was still one last choice I could make, I turned and threw myself off the precipice on which I stood. I prayed to Gua that perhaps there would be a river not too frozen for me to die in below.

But I never made it to that river. Instead, Rizel spread wings blacker than night and dug his talons into me, catching me midair. He flew with me like that—at his mercy, subject to his pain—until I was sure those talons would rip through my leg and my arm. When at last we landed, he hurled me into the snow. A dark cave stood behind me, and Rizel stood between me and any precipice that I could hurl myself over.

"In," he said, his voice tight with rage.

He will have to throw me into that cave. I will not go. I sat up in the snow, scarlet staining the white banks as my wounds bled. I looked Rizel in the eye. "Are you so angry, General Rizel, because I belong to Nkita? Or are you so filled with hate because a simple Grounded... bested you." I smiled at him, my fear urging me forward into recklessness. "I took everything you ever had, everything you ever worked for—your rank, your home, your power, your profession—with a single twisted lie. An easy one to tell. And not because I am brilliant. But because you were too stupid to think I could do it."

He rushed forward, that coward, and took my throat in his hands, squeezing until my eyes bulged. His talons scraped the back of my neck as he changed before my eyes. Fine fur in striations along his neck, vining up his face, his very pupils lengthening, his fangs enlarged for the kill. For a moment, I thought this was best. At least he would kill me quickly and be done with it. No torture in his sordid cave of a home.

But I was not ready to die. Just as I had not been ready to give Nkita's name to Letti. Despite the pain, despite the prospect of untellable agony...I wanted to live. To see him again.

Gua...I prayed. I prayed though blood dripped from my nose, from my eyes. *Gua...help the helpless.*

I heard no response. Gua did not speak like humans or Crylia. She did not form words with some filthy mouth. But I could feel her in the snow stuck to my frozen skin. I could hear her in the gentle forming of the icicles at the mouth of the cave.

Just then, a gurgle came from the mouth of the exiled General. And even though he fell to his knees, he refused to release me, his hand still clenching my throat.

Letti.

She peeled his fingers off me, one by one. I hacked into the snow, struggling to draw breath.

Rizel fell to his side, sinking his talons into Letti's ankle as he did so, forcing her to cry out in pain. I scrambled forward as she fell and found the knife she'd laid into the flesh between his wings. I pulled it out and drove it hard into his arm, twisting the blade until he had no choice but to release his grip on the gray wing.

She scurried backward, still clutching the cloth sack, her eyes wide, her breathing harried. "You!" she cried out.

"Letti...." but no other words could leave me. I coughed with effort.

"Stay away from me!" she screamed, her finger pointed at me, her eyes bloodshot. "Stay away!"

"Please...." I tried to speak, tried to reach for her. *What is she so afraid of? I would never harm her....*

But the gray wing hurled the sack at me when I inched forward. She crawled to the edge of the cliff and rolled off, her wings catching her before she could fall. I watched as she soared away from me, clearing a mountain peak in a matter of moments.

As quickly as I could, I took the blade from Rizel's arm.

He groaned and flailed, trying to take hold of me once more though his eyes were closed, his face buried in the snow.

With the blade in one hand, I grabbed the cloth sack and shoved it down the front of my dress. Then I stumbled inside Rizel's cave. I had little time. The Cryl would recover. *I could kill him,* I thought to myself. *I should kill him. Nkita wouldn't hesitate.*

But the thought of driving a blade into flesh once more—even if it was Crylia flesh—made my bones quake. So instead, I grabbed a second coat and a jar of pitch I saw sitting among Rizel's things. And I left, limping down the side of the mountain, regretting with each step that I did not take the life of the black wing I was leaving behind.

9

THE DAY THE SLAVER SPOKE

The wind beat the side of the mountain as I hid in the deepest crevice I could find, my sleeves over my face so I could gasp for air when the hail was not whipping in the bellows. There was no chance that Letti would come back for me this time. And I had no wings to carry me to safety, though I doubted even the strongest Cryl could fly in such a storm.

I did my best not to fall asleep by thinking of the warmest thoughts I could. Of the few years I'd had with my family before we were separated. Of the way my father winked at my mother when she made the stew he liked after a good catch of fish. Of mending nets beside my grandmother, me leaning against her round knee while she told stories of Gua and her goodness. I let these memories heat my soul until I had no choice but to drift to sleep.

When I awoke, I was being jostled in the back of an open wagon. Someone ran their hands over my arms and legs, warming me with strange heat.

I gasped, scrambling away, my back ramming into the rail of the wagon bed. My limbs burned when I moved them, but emerald eyes stared back. The gray wings had thick feathers along the tops of their shoulders and not just on their tucked wings.

Wait…I angled just a bit. No, they have no wings.

"You're…Grounded," I croaked.

The oldest male of the four in the back of the wagon nodded. "You too."

"But…you aren't wearing your ring," I said, touching my bottom lip to feel for mine. It too was gone. "Where is it?" Panic. Panic abundant, pulling my aching limbs back to life. Without my lip ring, it would be less likely that I would be immediately identified as Grounded. Which meant it would be less likely that I would be immediately identified as Crylia.

"They took them," the gray wing said. He had a strange way of speaking, but his wrinkled skin made him look kind enough. "Took our rings."

"But…why? And why am I here in this wagon? I was in Led—"

"Still in Led. In Lower Led."

In the valleys? I had never even heard of Lower Led. Perhaps the maps I'd studied before I left Tru were out of date. "Why are we in Lower Led?"

"To be sold."

Oh, Cryl be damned. Slavers. "Sold to where?"

The Cryl wrinkled his nose. "Don't know."

The female at his side sniffled, inching closer to him. "Gold wing will probably go to the Capital." She gestured to her own gray hair, but she was staring at my golden tresses and the hints of gold on my skin.

The male nodded. "Bet you'll be in a Teth house."

No. No, a Teth would know I was Nkita's mate. And they would turn me into the Cza. Which would bring Nkita running to save me.

"I have to get out of here," I whispered. I studied our speed as we rolled along. Not too fast. I could jump.

"We're all chained together," the male Cryl explained. "You'd have to take us with you."

"Well, let's go then," I snapped. "You can take your freedom when I take mine."

He shook his head. "Misery for runners."

"Misery I can handle. Going back to the Capital, I cannot."

"Back?"

I sighed. *Said too much.* "We need to find our rings and get out of here." *Or I will need the key to these shackles.* I located the metal against my ankle at last. There would be no wrenching my wrist out of place to escape.

The countryside rolled around us, a gloomy gray. Quiet snow fell along the dirt road, killing any hope for the deep green grass to survive. I refused to let it weaken my resolve. *But I will survive. I will.*

That was when I remembered. *The pitch!* I'd taken a jar of it on the mountain, but it was too snowy and the air too thin for me to light it. In the valley of Lower Led, though, there was plenty of air. And our wagon meant there was plenty of wood.

I rustled in my coat pocket and found the glass jar, then I dumped the pitch onto the wagon bed.

"What are you doing?" the gray wing asked.

"Hush," I chided. "And get ready."

I began to clank my chains together, working as fast as my clumsy hands could. I needed a spark. *One little spark. Just one—*

We came to a stop, and the slaver swung his legs to the ground. He was a burly Crylia. A white wing, but so filthy he might as well have been gray. I stuffed the pitch into my bodice with haste just as he grunted and pulled our chains, forcing us all to the ground.

My wounds threatened to tear open, but I dug my shaking heels into the muck, refusing to go along with the slaver until he yanked his chain up over his shoulder. My head banged on the ground as he urged the other Cryl to walk on.

A shoddy little cottage stood down the road. The closer we got to it, the harder I fought. I grabbed onto trees, raked my fingers into the sod.

Finally the slaver stopped. "What is wrong with you, female?" he huffed.

"I am not going to be a slave," I told him, panting with my elbows in the muck. "I won't."

"You will."

I sat up, rubbing my horribly bruised ankle. "How much will you earn for me, slaver?"

"None of your business—"

"I'll double it."

He smiled, one of his teeth missing. "No. Grounded have no gold."

"I can earn you more free than I ever would earn you if you sold me."

"So you want to be my slave?"

"I want to be your hire."

He scoffed. "To help me with my slaving or to help me with my member? I am not interested in marrying a Grounded muckeater."

"Your member holds none of my interest. What I mean is...I can get you information. And that information can get you anything you want."

"Enough talk, Grounded. Now walk along nicely, or I'll beat you down so you're easier to carry."

10

THE DAY THE CHAINS BROKE

Into a cage in the moldy little house at the end of the road. The slaver left me shackled to the other Grounded and pushed stale bread through the bars. I kept my eyes locked on him.

"You should take my offer," I said. "Believe me."

"Don't care what you say, Grounded. Slavemaster comes through and he'll pay me well for you. Done deal."

I tried once more. If I could get an amount, I would lie and say I could outbid it. "How much?"

"Shut your mouth now."

On my knees, I reached through the bars and grabbed the hem of his muddy trousers. I held on for dear life. "I can't go back," I said, trying to will him to release me. "I can't go back."

He yanked his leg away. And turned his back. And I did the last thing I knew to do.

"If you don't let me go, he'll come for me."

This did make the slaver stop. He returned, crouching before me on his massive haunches. "You already belong to another master, Grounded?"

I nodded. "I do. And he will come."

"Because you're such a special slave?"

"Because I'm *his*. And he doesn't share."

A grunt. "He's a Teth?"

"Grand Teth," I said. The elite of the elites. Tethered to the Cza since birth and elevated in service to him. Nkita was one, yes, but I could not use his name. So I lied. "Rizel."

"That General is exiled."

"To the mountains of Led. Which is where you found me, is it not?"

"Rizel cannot come to get you, though. I have nothing to fear."

"He will come, slaver."

"You are lying."

I swallowed. "Please—"

"Enough."

"I'd rather throw myself off an icy cliff than go back to working in the Capital."

But the slaver was gone.

The night came, and the gray wings pulled apart the stale loaf to pass around. I drifted to sleep, my head pressed against the bars, until the slavemaster came by and smacked his rod against the cell. He was tall and thin, a white wing with a grimace and squinting Crylia eyes. He counted us out and paused when he saw me.

"Gold wing, eh? The Cza is paying hefty for gold wings these days. Rare, they say."

The Cza was not paying because gold wings were rare. He was paying because he was looking for me. Because he was looking for my mate.

The slavemaster moved on, and I set myself to thinking. *I must escape...somehow. Some way.*

Another day passed, and the night fell heavier than the time before, the dark draping over us, hemming us in.

"Grounded." A whisper and a candle's light. The burly white wing slaver knelt before me once more.

"Slaver," I whispered back.

"The Cza is looking for gold wings."

"Alright...."

"Do you know *why* he's looking for gold wings?"

"We're...rare."

"Ah. You are. But you've always been rare, with your pretty shining wings. So why all of a sudden is the Cza paying more than ever before to find golds?"

"I—"

"Because there is a Grand Teth...gone missing." He held up a calloused finger. "A black wing General."

"Slaver—"

"Who married a gold wing Grounded—"

"That is a very entertaining story—"

"You're not Rizel's slave." He leaned in close, his wrinkled eyes searching me out. "I know who you belong to."

I inhaled, my breath shaking. *What do I say? What do I say?*

"We'll need a distraction, Lady Grounded."

I gasped. The only ones who ever called me Lady Grounded...were the rebels who freed us from the Cza's clutches. "A...distraction?"

"The *krov vanya crystin* will indeed be looking for his mate. And he can't very well find you in the Capital beneath the feet of that bloodplucked Cza. But I turn in my keys when I take my payment from the slavemaster. We need to give him a reason to open this cell."

"Cyndr!" the slavemaster called.

The slaver tapped on the bars. "With haste, Lady."

"Th-thank you...Cyndr."

"Anything for the Pureblood Heir and his mate."

"Syiva," I told him. "My name."

"Pleasantries later. Escape now."

He set his candle down and hurried off.

I turned to the gray wings. "Look alive, you huddling crew. We are getting out of here. Tonight."

"Out?"

"Out."

I reached into my dress front and pulled the pitch out, dropping it to the ground. Then, I reached through the bar and grabbed the candle. The fire roared to life, consuming the pitch, though it was damp, and eating away at the floorboards until the gray wings began to scream. And scream.

"My merchandise!" the slavemaster cried. "Cyndr! Take the keys!"

By merchandise he meant us. If we were burned, he could not sell us and he could not get his gold back from Cyndr either.

The slaver came clomping over, keys in hand. "Time to go," he said, swinging the bars open. "All of you."

But the gray wings wouldn't move. They stayed cowered together on the other side of the flames.

"We have to go," I said to them. "Now. Please."

But they refused to budge.

Cyndr reached down and grabbed onto the chain around my ankle. "I was not given the key to these shackles. If they will not come willingly, I will drag them, because I cannot leave you—"

"No!" I cried. "You cannot drag them through flames! They are not moving because they are *terrified*."

"They are not moving because they are prepared to be slaves."

I swallowed this. Defeat was clear on their faces, their ringless lips quivering. I tried one more time. "Come with us," I tried. "Come. Please."

But they refused.

I inhaled. "I would rather lose my leg than drag them through fire, slaver."

Cyndr roared with rage, his talons sprawling to life. Then the slaver brought those razors down against the chains while the flickering flames licked the hem of my dress. When at last the chain broke, Cyndr yanked me up by the arm. "We fly."

But one of the old gray wings—indeed the oldest Cryl I'd ever seen—hurled herself through the flames with a shriek, her hair and clothes lighting as she fell into my arms.

I patted her down, dousing the flames. Then I looked at Cyndr, my stare determined. "She's coming too."

He sighed. "Then, Lady Grounded...we run."

11

THE DAY THE OLD CRYL STAYED

For a Cryl in the middle of a sleepy Led valley, the slave-master certainly had a lot of guards at his disposal. He sent them out after us all at once, and though we were pummeling through the trees, we were doing so in the darkness. And they were gaining.

"Use your sight," Cyndr growled.

Of course, I did not have Crylsight to use. My eyes adjusted like human eyes did, slowly or not at all. Luckily, though it pained me to be thankful for another's misfortune, the old Cryl female stumbled, and I caught her elbow just before she tumbled down the side of the hill.

"We are going too fast for her," I said, my exhales heavy.

"Then we need to lose her," Cyndr replied.

"I am not leaving her behind. If the slavers capture her—"

"She is an old Grounded muckeat—"

"As far as I am concerned, this female is my *clan* now. And I am not leaving my clan mother behind." I balled my hands into fists, wishing I could square my stance, but feeling the soreness of my still-knitting wounds.

Cyndr thought, his shoulder heaving from exertion. Then, when he spoke, his tone changed. "Go on ahead. The both of you."

"Cyndr—"

"You cannot save everyone, Lady Grounded." He pointed his thick finger at me, looking up from beneath his hooded brow. "Remember that."

"I—"

"They are closing in. I will fight them off, but you must make it back to the Pureblood. He will need his mate if he is to save us from the Cza."

With a rush of resolve, I grabbed the hand of the old gray wing and stumbled off into the night.

We did not stop until there was no more breath in our lungs. I rested my back against a strong tree and sank down to the damp earth. My body shook with overexertion. It had already taken enough punishment working for Urol. My fight with Rizel and the treatment of the slaver did not strengthen me in any way.

When I awoke among light's earliest rays, it was to the gray wing female cooking something beneath the evergreen trees. I hurried forward, terrified that she had lit a smoke signal, that the slavers would follow it to find us. But no, she had dampened the smoke. *Clever old Cryl.* Most Crylia monsters I knew were detached from the old ways of how to live among the trees. Especially in the capital, they lived for their Vecherin, for their elegant balls and their decadent food and drink, their glittering pearls and glistening gems.

But not so with the older woodland Cryl, it seemed. Not so.

I approached the old Crylia, hunching down near the small fire, my hands over the warmth it gave. "You remind me of my grandmother," I told her. "She was always the best at making fires."

The old woman looked at me with perpetually wide eyes, her gaze like that of a swallow or a robin, her nose pointed almost like a beak. Her singed, wiry gray hair stood out in all directions on her head, her wrinkles like sharp lines cut into her leathery skin.

I wondered what she thought of me in the morning sun. Could she see the way my hair flowed wavy and gold from the roots, traces of white like the raging rapids Gua gave us? Could she tell that my breasts were too full for a Crylia female, that my skin was too soft and supple, that my nose did not hook quite enough? That my fingertips had nowhere for talons to hide?

I prayed she could not see me. That she could only see a Grounded gold wing.

But then I realized...she'd heard Cyndr speak of the Pureblood Heir. Which means, like it or not, this female was a liability to both Nkita and me. I would have to keep her close.

But where are we going? I had no plans, no direction. I didn't even know where Nkita was at this point, so how could I avoid him?

"We...should get going," I told the old one.

But she just stabbed her twig into the fish cooking on the fire and handed it to me. It was roasted to perfection, and the realization of how devastatingly hungry I was brought me to my knees. We shared the fish, and the old female smiled as I devoured her cooking.

"Do...you speak, Mother Cryl?" I asked her.

She only beamed at me. But when she turned her head, I caught sight of a few blisters on the side of her face. I knew what our next mission would be right then.

"We will get you some medicine," I explained. "And then perhaps we will travel deeper into Led."

She reached out and touched my bottom lip, her brow creased.

Cryl be damned. "We have no rings." I sat in the dirt, nibbling on what was left of my fish and thinking. "We must acquire some rings before we can get medicine. So now we are on two missions. Does that sound alright?"

She nodded, and I followed my ears to an icy creek nearby to have a drink and to clean the mud off me as best I could. I swore, out of the corner of my eye, that I saw something move. A figure. Maybe even a Crylia. But when I looked there was nothing to see except the glory of sunrise shifting through the canopies. Yet the clouds were gathering, gray and gray piling together, filling the sky. Soon they would own the sky. *A storm comes.*

And I felt a storm brewing in my very soul as well. 'Storms are warnings' said the teachings of Gua.

Something is coming.

12

The Day The Rebel Returned

"What do I call you?" I asked the old gray wing. "How will I know your name if you cannot tell me?"

She gave me a toothless smile as a response.

I grinned back. "That's an expression, not a name. I can't very well call to you by smiling across the forest, now can I?" I peeked out from our hiding place among the trees. We were spying on the village we'd come across to make sure there were no slavers and no Capital white wings milling about.

"I'm Oahra," I offered. *I should have chosen a different name, though. Perhaps it sounds a bit too Tru, especially when I say it.* My tongue was well practiced in the short, clipping sounds of Crylia speech. Especially for the females, the Crylia often spoke in shrill, chirping tones.

Humans had many different languages, but Tru speech was very distinct among the tribes. Every so often, I slipped back into old habits without realizing it, my vowels long and round and heavy, like I was humming a song.

In Cryl common tongue, my new name should have been pronounced 'hwa-duh', the syllables rushing together, the sound of the 'd' harsh.

If I slipped into my native tongue, however, Oahra would be drawn out, each syllable savored, the 'r' gentle. 'O-ah-rah'. With a great deal of breath behind each sound, like the wind rippling the surface of a great sea—

The old Cryl elbowed me out of my thoughts.

"Oahra," I said again, this time in perfect Cryl common tongue. "And maybe we will call you...Drosya." *For wisdom and courage.* Both of which the old one had displayed in plentiful quantities in the five days since we'd been traveling together.

"I much enjoy your company, Drosya," I told her. "It is better than being beaten in taverns or beaten in servant quarters or...beaten."

Drosya nodded her head in affirmation, sticking her tongue out at me.

"But we need this medicine for your blisters. They are not healing as they should. And we need new rings. Or we will both be in trouble if we are found out. So...I will sneak into this village to obtain them. And you can wait here for me behind these trees. No fires this time, please. I need you to be able to run away quickly if anyone comes through who is not me."

I chewed on my lip, surprised to find no ring there. It had been so long since my people had shoved the needle through, I forgot what it was like to be without a Grounded ring. "Perhaps I should hide you, Drosya. That way you can rest while you wait for me." I pointed to a wide tree with enormous, knotted roots.

I nestled Drosya in and hoisted some dried branches to cover her. To my great surprise, she tapped her index finger to the center of her forehead before I lowered the last bit of foliage.

It was a custom I had to see among the Crylia. We Tru usually did it to ask for Gua's blessing. I wondered what the motion meant to Drosya. Or...perhaps her forehead was simply itchy. *Woodland Cryl are a strange breed, that is for certain.*

I moved carefully into the village, wishing that I had at least a cloak with which to cover my tattered dress and my amble bruises and scrapes. But the slavers had taken the coat Letti gave me, so I had to make do.

The village was small and crowded, the Cryl inside it ornery and bathed in grime. Cries of 'Cza be damned' and 'Down with the King' filled the filthy streets. Some Cryl laid their sick out on the corners, clustered together and coughing and shuddering. Rarely had I seen ill Crylia in the Capital. There were none. It was unheard of. But here in the outskirts of Led, illness was as common as gray wings.

"Move, or I'll set you to roosting!" someone snarled, shoving me out of the way as he pushed his cart of spoiled berries and squash.

I wanted to find a smithy, but I knew better than to ask any of the grimacing males. And most of the females looked just as wrathful. So I sneaked my way to a small Crylia offspring and whispered, "The smithy?"

She held out her hand for coin. I cursed myself for not asking Cyndr for some when we parted ways. I shook my head no, and the offspring spit in my face.

So much for that idea.

I scrubbed at my cheek and wandered until I found the shop myself. The gray wing smithy had his back turned to any potential customers, hammering away at some metal thing, no doubt, his wings tucked.

"Excuse me," I said, keeping my voice timid, as was befitting to my station. "Excuse me, good smithy?"

"I don't take work requests from *females*," the smithy roared, refusing to even look my way.

But...I knew that voice.

It was the voice of the rebel Cryl who'd pulled Nkita and me from the raging river outside the Cza's Castle. Who found us refuge in a woodland town. Who hauled deer home every day when Nkita healed from the loss of his wing at the hands of the King.

Hrogar.

13

THE DAY THE TRU FELL

I scrambled away, bumping into a limping Crylia behind me. I offered my apologies, but he cursed loudly anyway. Then he began to look me over, his brows hoisted and his eyes narrowed.

I ducked my head to keep him from seeing my missing ring and tried not to run to the other side of the village. *So much for getting those rings the easy way.* I clenched my fists, trying to calm myself. *I need to return to the trees, get Drosya, and run.*

I made it to the edge of town, hoping to sneak into the treeline and make my way back through the forest to Drosya's hiding place. But a female cut off my progress. She yanked my arm, pulling me toward her with her feeble strength.

"You in need of work, Grounded?"

Not the sort of work she would be offering, no. "I am ill," I lied, hoping she would release me.

She hauled up, spitting out her phlegm. "You'll be letting the Master make that call. He doesn't mind if you've got scabs, as long as you can spread your knees and keep your voice down." Then, she tilted her head and called, "Come! Take this one to the master!"

A young gray wing responded, though he was twice my width, his knuckles bruised from a life of swinging his fists. He took hold of my wrist without hesitation.

Oh, Cryl be damned. I will have to fight.

Any combat skills I'd learned from the Tru would be useless, not only because I would be found out as human, but also because the Cryl had dominated us in war for as long as war had existed. But Nkita taught me enough of Cryl combat for me to at least resist this coercion, even if it was just for a few moments. My efforts had proven useless against Cyndr, but maybe this young Cryl was prideful enough to be caught off guard.

I twisted my arm free of the gray wing and brought the side of my boot down with all my force into the top of his knee cap until it cracked.

He howled, and I darted away, trying to make for the trees. But the Crylia surged forward, gripping my ankle so that I fell sharply, smacking my elbows on the street.

I meant to scream when he shoved my face down with his strong palm, his talons showing themselves. But suddenly, the pain ended. I heard a whimper and then a plop, like a sack hitting the ground. And in my daze, I remembered the first time I met my General. He had landed with all his peril, dropping his bundle of weapons to the ground and looking dead at me. He'd loved me from that moment, he always told me.

"Up," said a smooth, deep voice. And I was pulled to my feet in one rush.

The young Cryl lay in a heap, his throat crushed and his eyes pooling with blood. Dead. The female who'd tried to recruit me for her master hid behind the wall of their squat little building.

"Breathe."

I looked up to the one who spoke. Dark hair grown out to his chest, sharp features as if he were carved from the side of a Led mountain. And one black wing full-spread behind him.

I didn't know what to say. I didn't know what to do. I...didn't know who to be.

Nkita put a hand to my cheek. "Are you able to move?" he asked, his voice surrounding me.

I nodded. My legs could work, though I had no idea how I could get them to obey me. When I did not move, Nkita pressed me against him and moved on my behalf, *Gua help the helpless*, carrying both of us through to the treeline.

He stopped when we were deep in the forest, setting me to the ground on shaky legs.

"You need water," he said.

But I clutched the sleeves of his shirt, refusing to let go of him. *Release him, Em*, I told myself. *You don't want him to think you need him. You are fine. You're just fine without him.* But my grip would not loosen, my fists would not uncurl.

Nkita held me to him once again, moving his arms out of my grasp so he could pull me tighter and tighter against his chest and so I could bury my face against his dark shirt. He said nothing for a time. Only held me that way until I could breathe again. Until my heart slowed and beat like his, in rhythm. I swore even our blood flowed through our veins in harmony.

"I found you," he whispered at last. "It's alright now."

He found me.

I wanted to say something. To tell him that I didn't want to be found. That I had done all this, endured all this for so long, to keep from him holding me like this, to stop him from whispering against my hair, to prevent him from forcing me to fall in love over and over.

But only tears slipped from my eyes, and I couldn't very well let the great Grand Teth General see those. Or he would know. He would know I wanted him to come chasing me down. That I wanted him to fight through sleepless nights, refusing to accept I was gone for good.

So I buried my tears in his embrace, hiding myself once more. If he knew—if he knew how much I loved him— he would be more than enraged. He would be vigilant. And I would never be rid of the General ever again.

14

The Day The General Took Hold

"We must keep moving. For now," Nkita said.

My whole body echoed with the fullness of his voice, even though he spoke barely above a whisper. I nodded my head, glad that my eyes were still closed. I hoped I never had to look at him again. That I could avoid his gaze for the rest of my life. What it held for me, I could not bear to discover.

"Come on," he told me. And then he hoisted me up, my legs wrapping around his waist. "Rest a while. I will carry you."

"We have to go back. To the other side of town," I croaked.

"We cannot. We must make distance between us and Hrogar before it is too late."

I have my reasons for fleeing from Hrogar, but what are Nkita's? But there was no time to ask such questions.

"Nkita. I left a comrade hiding in the trees. I cannot...
I cannot abandon her."

"She will make her own way—"

"*No.*"

"Emyri—"

"Oahra," I corrected him. "My name to the woodland
Crylia is Oahra. And if you do not circle back for her,
I will never forgive you."

He scoffed. "It is not *you* who can withhold forgiveness. And I *don't care* what you tell Cryl you are called.
I will call you Em. I will call you your *name*."

"But—"

"It is not *subject* to your *approval*," he snapped.

But he did turn back, circling the town through the
trees. If he had both his wings, perhaps we would have
taken to the air. But he lost his gift of flight the day the
Cza ripped his wing from his back. And instead...all
First General Nkita was left with...was me.

"There," I told him. I pointed to the great tree with the
winding roots. "She is there. Hiding among the branches."

I slipped down from Nkita's arms and limped over to
the place where I'd left Drosya, kneeling and tossing the
branches aside. But...she was gone.

"Drosya?" I stood to my feet, my heart trembling.
*Someone has taken her. A slaver or—or worse. But they
put the branches back in place? Why? How?* "Drosya!"

Nkita grabbed my arm. "Em, keep your voice down."

"I have to find her."

"We are out of time—"

"You don't *understand*, Nkita!" My eyes filled with tears. "She is old and Grounded and she doesn't even have her ring. She doesn't *speak*! And she's...she's alone. I cannot leave her."

"If she is old, she will never be able to keep up anyway. We must move quickly."

"I was supposed to be getting us rings. And medicine for her burns. She—"

Nkita put his thumb to my bottom lip, where my silver ring should have been. "Where did yours go?"

"Slavers. But—"

I did not have to look at him to feel his mood shift, to hear the rustling of feathers. He was beyond furious. But fury would not find Drosya.

"We need to look for her."

"If you do not come with me now, I will pick you up and put you over my shoulder, Emyri Izela. And your choice to cooperate will be removed from you."

I walked away from him, studying the ground for traces, for tracks, for any clues as to where Drosya might have gone and why. I even sniffed the air, hoping to smell roasting fish from her clever little fires. *Gua. Gua, please. Help the helpless. Help me find her.*

In one fluid movement, with more strength than any human could possess, Nkita lifted me onto his shoulders. All I could see was the black of his trousers and the hem of his shirt, the mud caked onto his midnight boots and the hilt of his sword. And of course the taut, roundness of his rear as he stomped forward.

I tried to cry out, but he refused to hear me. And there was no loosening his grasp on me. Not until we'd traveled enough distance that I could never find my way back to that tree.

It was nightfall by the time my mate set me down on my own two feet. I roared with rage, shoving his chest with all my strength.

"You had no right!" I cried. I had never felt so much shame at being forced, not even when Cyndr dragged me through the muck.

Nkita did not care that I thumped away at him. "I have every right, Em. And I will have every right from now until your last breath."

Hot tears of anger blurred my vision. "I am not some object to be hoisted and dragged about! I am a human being. I am owed dignity. And the ability to choose for myself where my body goes and what it will do!" I shoved him again. It would have been more effective if I could have budged him even an inch. "I am Emyri of the Tru. And I am not your *possession*, Nkita."

He spoke so coolly that the air between us nearly froze. "I don't give a *damn*."

I sniffled, a new wave of icy rage flooding me. "What did you just say to me?"

"I don't give a damn what you think you're owed. I don't *give. A. Damn*."

My jaw dropped. *This from the Cryl who told me I was good? That I deserved to see myself as I truly was?* "You don't think I am owed...dignity, Nkita?"

Without warning, the black wing moved forward, his eyes locked onto mine—my mistake for looking at him at last—and shadows exuding from his very soul. He walked until I had no choice but to press my back against a tree, the bark pinching my weary skin, my breath leaving me with every shiver. Nkita put his hand around my slender throat. He did not squeeze, as Rizel had. But he spoke with a voice that could not be denied.

"You are wondering where your dignity has run off to? I saw that stripped away the day the Great Cza laid you on your back and forced me to enter you before the Teth. I saw it ripped to shreds when you wept every time I returned to you alive after battle. I saw it crushed to nothing but dust when that same King tore my wing from my very spine." He waited, breathing in when I could not bring myself to breath out. There was no compassion in those lilac eyes this time. "Put your hand where it *belongs*, Em."

I swallowed and slowly, as if I were reaching toward an open flame, I curled my fingers against his neck. We held there, mirroring each other, staring into one another's eyes, until I was not sure I could stand any longer.

"I will not see your dignity touched again, Emyri Izela. Not by Cryl, not by Tru, not by slavers, not by the Cza of Crylia—"

"And not by *you*?"

He narrowed those glittering eyes. "You truly find offense?"

I wished to raise my voice above a whisper, but there was no strength left in my words. "Yes."

"Then I have wronged you."

"You have."

"And you have wronged me."

"I—"

"You have wronged me." His voice rang out, shaking the leaves of the trees, threatening the darkness.

I gasped, tears slipping at last down my filthy cheeks. "Yes."

"We will earn each other's forgiveness then. In time."

Even in my exhaustion, I wanted him. For his hand to trail down to my chest, for him to take hold of me as he did that first night at the Vecherin.

For a moment, I was certain he wanted me as well. Something about the way the veins in his neck throbbed beneath my fingers. The way his breath caught when he inhaled. How his lips parted when he leaned in closer to me ever so slightly.

But he released me just as quickly as he'd held my throat tight. And when Nkita turned away, a fear I never thought would be mine took hold of me instead.

I tried to lose him...and it worked. A shudder took me to my knees. *I've lost my mate.*

15

THE DAY THE FIRE SPARKED

Another branch clattered to the forest floor, joining the pile of wood destined for oblivion. Nkita said nothing as he added to the stack. The fish he'd caught hung from a string tied to the bough of a tree. His silent work was efficient, as if he moved from muscle memory. I wanted to ask him how many times he'd survived off the land like this while he was hunting my people in the war. But I decided against it. Such a question would seem antagonistic. And we needed no more tension between us, that much was certain.

He insisted I rest, so I leaned back against a tree, twiddling my thumbs and staring at his movements. His hands were sure, confident as they cracked bigger branches into pieces to add to the pile. I knew the exact feel of those hands. It was not so bad to be broken by them.

He set to starting the fire, and I cleared my throat, hoping to get Nkita's attention. When it did not work, I tried again. Then again.

Finally, kneeling in the dirt, he turned to me. "What's wrong with you?"

I nodded my chin toward the kindling. "You'll set off smoke with an open fire like that."

He narrowed his eyes at me. "I know how to make fire, Em."

"That much is clear. But it is also clear that you know how to make smoke. Because that is what you're about to do."

"And you know how to make fire without smoke? Your goddess teach you that?"

I more than bristled. "Do not speak Gua's name irreverently."

"I didn't speak her name at all."

"I am serious, Nkita. Just because the Cryl have no religion—"

"Worship is for the weak, Em. I am not going to apologize for us being too strong for it."

"I am not asking for an apology. I am asking you to leave the mention of Gua out of your mouth."

He glared at me, his gaze refusing to soften. "I will remain *silent*, then."

"Cryl be damned, Nkita. Your arrogance is infuriating." I brought myself to my feet, and he growled, for I was supposed to be resting. "Hush. I will show you how the

Tru make quiet fires whether your pride gives me permission or not."

I gathered nearby stones, the flatter the better, and when I moved for a large one, Nkita growled once more, snatching it from me and carrying it himself to the kindling. In fact, every time I found a new stone, he took it from me and left me standing with empty hands.

Finally, I knelt beside the fire, arranging the stones in a pattern. "Build the fire like a river," I explained.

"You can't build rivers."

I rolled my eyes at the General. "Crylia think they know everything. But we build rivers all the time. Even as children, we practiced the art. My closest friend was a river builder once." I bit my tongue at the mention of friends. Such days were far behind me. And I did not want my mate asking questions about my past. "The fire flows through the guide stones, just as water would. And so there is no gathering of smoke. Gua teaches all things when she brings the water."

When I looked up, Nkita was not observing my lesson. He was observing me.

"What is it?" I asked.

"Strange."

I blushed, self conscious as he continued to stare. "What is strange?"

"Strange to hear you speak of your ways so openly. We had to hide before."

I made a note to myself to speak of them less. "Now you can light it, and no one will track us through the smoke lifting above the trees." I went to gather the fish, but Nkita spoke out.

"That's enough. Go rest."

"But—"

"If we have to run, you will need strength. Sit down, woman."

I remained standing, observing as he prepared the fish and lowered them into the flames.

"Your obstinance is idiotic," Nkita grumbled when I did not obey him.

"We have to go back."

"Let the old Cryl out of your head, Em."

I inhaled, filling myself with courage and hoping that would be translated to something communicable. "Nkita Opas. When I ran, there was someone who said she would help me. And at the very first opportunity, she sold me out and left me for worse than dead."

My skin prickled as his attitude shifted. He moved from relatively irritated to intensely protective. Almost predatory. It frightened me that I could sense this shift while knowing it was not my own emotion I felt.

"Give me her name," he whispered, his fists clenched.

"Drosya Gray Wing."

He rose. "She will be found—"

"Drosya is the name I gave the old Crylia. The one *I* left behind for worse than dead. If you would so readily seek out someone who wronged me, do not let me be in the wrong."

I waited, letting that make its way through Nkita's mind. His shoulders relaxed, but his frown did not lift. "If we go back, we will end up with Hrogar again. He is difficult to lose, and I cannot very well kill him."

"No, it would not do well to kill the rebel aid. Politically, it will seem you are against the rebels, and we need their protection from the Cza." Hrogar was unpleasant, but he and Rhaza had worked together to save us from the Cza's Castle. And Cyndr had saved me from the cold of Led and from the slavemaster's keep. We needed the alliance of the rebels or we would be in the Cza's clutches in a week's time.

"You misunderstand me. Perhaps willfully."

I scrunched my brow. "It's not willful. What do I not see?"

"You know nothing of black wings, it seems. I have behaved myself but I can only take so much, Em. If Hrogar disrespects you and I let myself so much as exhale, I will crack his spine into a dozen pieces. And then what?"

So...I am the problem. Again. Already. "I will go back for Drosya alone—"

Nkita narrowed his eyes at me. "*Stop.*"

"Alright."

"We can go up a few miles to a town I know. We will be safe for a time, and I can acquire a new ring for you.

Some clothes. A bed. Then we can make plans for how to locate your liability."

"A bed?" I asked him as he handed me a share of roasted fish.

He did not answer me, and I bit my lip to keep from making a sound that would give away how I felt at even the idea of being close to him. *Want him less, Em. It will be easier for you both if you want him less.*

"More."

I gasped. *He knows my thoughts now, this black wing? Gua help me!* "W-what?"

"Food. You should have more."

I swallowed. "Oh." I thought for a moment. "Nkita... can you...?" *Can he know my thoughts?*

"Can I what?"

I shook my head. "Can you pass me more fish?"

He approached with more of the meal, lilac eyes shining even though his stern features never changed. "Good," he said. "Now...more."

16

THE DAY THE ARROW FLEW

As we approached the cabin tucked in the forest trees, new snowflakes sprang from the clouds, drifting down in intricate spirals.

"It will storm," Nkita said, dusting the piles of snow from my hair. "We should see if he's home."

The cabin appeared to be sturdy, smoke curling from the chimney. Strange to be searching for an acquaintance of a Grand Teth in the middle of nowhere. All of Nkita's friends I'd met before were wealthy Teth and Generals or Teth-wed females with pearls embedded into their skin and crystals dangling from their eyelashes. But Nkita once again proved to be surprising. His friend lived on the outskirts of Led, and we pushed our way near the border of Crylia and Tru once more.

"Seems he is in," I said, pointing to the plumes. The faster we could get 'rest' and get this over with, the sooner we could leave the borderlands.

Nkita shook his head. "He keeps his fires lit whether the cabin is vacant or not."

"So...he is being hunted as well? And *this* is where we're choosing to hide out?"

Nkita's eyes changed, his pupils moving from spheres to slivers as his Crylsight came to life. "Be warned. He will either welcome me or try to kill me," he explained.

"*Kill* you, Nkita?"

He nodded. "And take you afterward."

"I thought you wanted me protected?"

Nkita scoffed. "I didn't say I would let him, Em. Have you no faith in me at all? Either way, we will use his cabin." He put his fingers to his lips and let out a series of whistles. When Crylia did this, they sounded exactly like eagles. So different from their lionesque growl or the hiss of their serpent spirit. That shrill eagle cry used to send ripples of fear through me. But when it came from Nkita...I had no worry for my safety.

"Come," he said. "He's not here." Nkita crept forward, his knees bent and his arm out to keep me behind him.

"If he's not here, why are we sneaking?"

Nkita held up a finger, then stretched his arm up high. In an instant, an arrow came hurtling through the air, leaving the cracked window of the cabin and nesting itself in the silver bark of a tree behind us.

"He likes traps."

Nkita stood after that, opening the door and shielding me with his arm once more as an axe thudded to the wooden planks beside our boots.

"Cryl be damned," I mumbled. "We might not make it through the night at this rate."

"We'll make it." Nkita took my hand and led me over the threshold of the door.

I blushed, my knuckles tingling beneath his touch. "What are you doing?"

"What do you mean?"

"Why are you holding my hand like this?"

Nkita shrugged. "We're wed. That's how I am supposed to enter rooms with you. Is that not one of your customs?"

"It is not." When he released my hand, I curled my fingers into a fist, savoring what lingered of the sensation. "You didn't do that before, when we were with Hrogar."

"Because we were with Hrogar. And he did not need to know."

I swallowed. "Did not need to know what?"

"That I meant it when I married you. That I mean it now."

My cheeks and chest flushed with heat, and I blamed it on the crackling of the fire. *Anything to keep from admitting that I also meant it. That I will always mean it.*

I walked around the small space, taking in the sight of the cabin. It was larger than Hrogar's and clean enough, though the furniture was sparse. The curtains were plain strips of dark cloth, and the table and chairs looked like they'd never been used.

"Do you think he has a bath?" I asked.

"It's out back. I'll show you."

"I am sure I'm clever enough to navigate the simple mechanics of a bath, Nkita."

"Weren't clever enough to navigate the simple location of one."

I glared at him. "What will I wear? Does he have a mate who might have clothes to spare?"

"No. Red wings don't wed. You should remember that, Em, or Cryl will know you're human."

"Oh? Is that how it works? If I don't know the right facts I will be found out? Thank you for explaining my own situation to me, great and noble Grand Teth Nkita."

Nkita kept his livid stare paired with mine as he removed his shirt and dangled it in front of me. "Your 'clothes to spare'."

I snatched it from him and made my way through the cabin, hesitating before I creaked the back door open, lest some arrow be sent flying. But nothing happened, and I found a simple metal basin filled with water. The top layer had already turned to ice, so I found a palm-sized rock and smashed through it.

There were no other houses, no company besides the deer that licked salt off the tree bark in the distance. And so I stripped off what was left in my dress and counted to three. The freezing water sliced through me, pain rearranging my senses. But I would be alright. It was water after all, and the goddess would be with me.

"I need to find you food," Nkita said, startling me as he stepped through the door.

Without his shirt, I had a clear, unimpeded view of his chest. The last time I had seen it, we laid together on the floor of my little prison in the Castle. He'd come back from battles, and I would examine his scars, old and new, and hear him tell me of his struggles. I wanted nothing more than to have him stay with me in those moments. But every time, he was ripped away, sent back to fight against my people.

"I am not too hungry," I lied, biting my lips to keep my teeth from chattering. The fish had kept me, but we both knew it was not enough.

"I will go regardless. But I need to know you will not run off."

"Nkita—"

"Emyri. Do not tell me more lies. I am tired of them. And I will not be the sort of mate who chains up his partner so she does what he wants. So just...stay. For half an hour while I catch something. Will you do that?"

I could not help but to stare at those scars twisting along his chest, at the way they weaved across his muscles, telling the stories of what he'd done to harm my kind— and to save it.

I nodded. "I will stay."

"And if Dagon comes while I am away—"

"You are leaving me with your sword?"

He shook his head. "Just scream. If you try to fight him, I will have to embark on a quest to avenge your death, and I'm too hungry for that right now."

I grinned. "Selfish."

"Always."

17

THE DAY THE CRYLIA STOPPED

"I'm quite surprised Dagon keeps salt in his pantry," Nkita said, chewing carefully. "He is not usually one for the finer things."

I stretched past him to grab another leg of squirrel and he slid one hand over my lower back as I did so, which made me drop not only the squirrel, but the entire platter onto the ground.

Nkita didn't seem to care that it was gone.

I meant to sit back down, but he twisted me and pushed me back so that my rear rested on the table top before him. Then, he dragged his chair forward until my knees had no choice but to part. And since I wore only his shirt, there was no mystery remaining between us.

I licked the salt off one of my fingers, but Nkita scowled and grabbed my hand. "It's not proper to do that."

"It's my meal. And they're my fingers." I shrugged. "No one is watching." I pretended I didn't want to squirm, what with my thighs resting against his ribs.

I went to savor the remaining fingers, but Nkita held firm to my wrist. I had to wrench it away to get myself free. Then, I licked each one, refusing to feel any semblance of shame.

He stared me down as I did it. "Are you finished?"

"If I must be—"

But he stood with such purpose that I gasped. "I want permission," he said.

"I—"

"Will you give it?"

I had to clear my throat twice, anticipation running up and down my spine, forcing my muscles to seize. "You don't have to keep asking. We—"

"I will always ask. Every time. Because you deserve the right to withhold. And...."

Breathe. Em, breathe. "And?"

He moved in closer so that I could feel his breath on my lips, so I could sense his desire as he inhaled, willing me closer. But he did not kiss me. "And I like to hear you say 'yes' to me, little spy."

I waited as he waited. I studied the cut of his clavicle, the throbbing of veins trailing up his neck. The thudding of his heart shook his chest, but the more ready he became, the slower that heart moved, until I wasn't sure it beat at all. As for mine...it raced with such abandon that I was sure he could see it rattling his shirt against my frame.

"Go ahead," he whispered.

I didn't realize I'd outstretched my hand until he leaned forward, pressing his chest to my open palm. His pores formed tiny knots beneath my fingertips as I moved my hand along his body.

"You're not angry with me?" I asked him, my voice little more than a gurgle in the back of my throat. "I thought you would be...furious."

"I am."

"But—?"

"I'll make you *pay*," he said simply.

I couldn't keep the corner of my mouth from twitching. "With my permission?"

Nkita reached forward and grabbed the back of my neck, dragging me so close to him that there was no space between our hips at all. His fingers dug into my spine hard enough to make me inhale, a murmur of surprise escaping my mouth. "You mistake my consideration for patience."

At any point in my young life, had someone told me I would want or crave or desire or need the sworn enemy of my people to touch every part of me...I would have called the healers and had their mind examined. But there I was, my body prickling, my soul demanding I say yes.

"You have my perm—"

Nkita's mouth was on mine in less than a moment. He drank deeply, as if he had been holding on for his life. Then, he plucked at the skin of my neck, my shoulder, carving my body with sharp teeth and quick lips. When I squirmed, he put a hand on my chest, pushing me so my back hit the table. The grain of the wood caught on the fabric of my shirt, but every sensation only made me more aware of how truly alive I felt.

A shadow cast over me when his black wing stretched full, no longer tucked behind Nkita's back. The darkness of the small room made his feathers appear to be dipped in pure ink, no gold shimmering among the onyx this time. The red and gold light of the fire danced on his features, so it seemed his stern face was hidden and revealed over and over again.

"Nkita—"

He gripped my thigh hard with one hand, and my words died on my tongue, his other hand slowly unfurling between my legs. "You misunderstand what is happening here," he explained. "You have one job. And it is to feel very, very sorry." He pressed deeper until I couldn't tell whether I wanted to wiggle away or slide in closer to his touch. "If you insist I stop, *dear mate*, you only need to wish it." He leaned in, still working. "I am *inside* you, Emyri Izela, in more ways than one. Did you know that?"

I gripped his wrist, though I could not say why I did it. *What...is he thinking? Does he not want to enter me truly? Does he not—*

He did not. He had no intention of satisfying himself. In fact, I believed my mate had no intention of satisfying me either. He watched carefully, his eyes devouring every change in me. The flushing of my skin, the quickening of my breath, the perspiration glistening on my chest, my thighs.

Until there was no more time, until there was no more anticipation. I could hold no more sensations in my body, my back about to arch, my muscles about to tighten.

That was when Nkita pulled his hand away. He straightened up, wiping his fingers in the hem of the shirt he'd lent me, his lilac eyes dancing as he watched me groan involuntarily.

His voice was so deep it made me shiver. "No more for you," he said. He took a fistful of the shirt, pulling me off the table and onto the floor in one motion. Then, he kissed my forehead and walked out the door.

18

THE DAY THE TROUBLE BEGAN

I followed Nkita outside, grateful that he could not escape me through flight. With the snow falling heavy and the clouds hiding the light of the sun, I stood just outside the cabin door. My bare feet burned from the frigid ice already forming on the little wooden porch. But I could put up with the pain. Anger fuels courage.

"*Nkita Opas!*"

My mate halted, calf-deep in the snow, and turned to face me. "Well now. The hypocrite calls."

"Come back here!"

"If only I could have said that to *you*, Em. But you never gave me the chance, did you?"

I crossed my arms against the cold. "I understand why you're upset, Nkita. I do," I shouted across the space between us, the whipping wind echoing my words as the storm increased in its intensity. "But I did the right thing when I ran, and you know it. It wasn't what you wanted but it was the only option I had. And now, you are punishing me for it. That isn't fair!"

He stomped back toward me, his body temperature changing to keep him warm while I forced myself not to shiver. When he made it to me, we stood face to face. His tone changed, and for the first time since he'd found me in that town, he sounded like himself. Honest, and not vindictive. More vulnerable than he let on. "You left me, Em."

"They were going to find us together, Nkita. And then—"

"You left me."

"And then they would put the pieces together. They would know we were the ones the Cza was looking for. A gold wing Grounded and a black wing Cryl with only one—"

"But you *left me*."

"I cannot do it again, Nkita! When you told me I would be your weakness, that I would be your downfall...I thought you were being dramatic! I did not know you meant it—"

"I told you I am always serious!"

"And I did not believe you. How could I believe you? Why would someone like you—someone powerful and... and monstrous and beautiful and frightening—choose to tie yourself to a liability? It makes no sense and it will never make sense. I did not believe you then and I will never be able to understand it. I didn't believe you...and that is *my* fault. Your wing, your rank, your *pain*—it's *my fault!*"

Nkita took my face in his hands and tilted my head up. The closer he came to me, the warmer he made me. "Emyri. What happened in the Castle was not your fault."

A sob crept its way through my body. "He used me to destroy you—"

"No." He kissed my forehead. "This is not about the King. It is about you and me. And, Em...Here is the truth. *You* gave me something worth losing. And when you left me...Em, what would remain for me? To live a miserable life alone? With...*with Hrogar*? Who would I argue with? Who would I scold, hm?"

I shuddered as I inhaled. Truth slipped from my lips to match his. "When I am with you, I am reminded of how easy it would be to lose you."

"And when I am with you, I am reminded of how difficult it will be to keep you."

"So...." I put my hand on his, my soul still wrestling with my heart, wanting to stay, wanting to go. Wanting to be his delight, to be his destruction. "We will struggle, then. Maybe forever."

"I look forward to a lifetime of utter aggravation."

This time, when the General kissed me, it was slow. Precise. But he pulled away, his hand curling around my back as he narrowed his eyes. "Stay close."

The hairs on his arms raised, his skin prickling beneath my touch. I clamped my mouth shut out of instinct.

"No, keep speaking to me like all is well," he whispered, tucking strands of my golden hair behind my ear. But he was far off, his focus on the sounds around us as I mumbled about Old Zloy and how she used to make me split the firewood for the whole house when I worked for Nkita.

"I'm going to walk you inside," he whispered, pretending he was kissing my temple, his lips brushing me as he continued to speak. "Get down on the ground and stay small until it's over. If I fall, you run through the back."

"If you fall?" I tightened my grip on his arm, my fingernails digging into him.

He stared at me, lavender eyes unwavering. "You think I could ever lose, Em?"

"You had better not, General."

"Yes, commander." The corner of his lips twitched. "Ready?"

I pretended to laugh and smacked his shoulder as if he were teasing me. "Of course," I said, searching out his eyes and finding no hint of fear. Whatever threat was coming—whoever Nkita heard—we would survive. Together. I released my breath slowly. "Ready."

19

THE DAY THE MONSTER CAME

Inside, the warmth of the fire attacked my frozen limbs. But there was no time to enjoy the heat. Not when Nkita closed the door behind us and then threw the table across the small room.

"Behind it," he said. "Now."

I scrambled to my knees, hidden between the overturned table and the wall. I heard the metallic ring of Nkita's sword as he withdrew it, followed by the crash of the door breaking down. A grunt as Nkita moved, his boots scraping against the wooden planks beneath him. Whoever he battled was quick, his sword whooshing and his grunts coming one after the other. I peeked out from behind the table.

A red wing.

He was beautiful, his long hair flying about his face in thick, wild locs. His face displayed countless scars, all healed scarlet to match his hair and brows. And his wings—fullspread, crimson with sprinkles of white, like the snow had landed on his wings and never melted. He was a bit thinner than Nkita, and it made him faster. He slashed his blade with a maniacal grin on his face, his nostrils flared, his tongue lagging when he needed to catch his breath. He wore a dark brown coat stitched of leather and felt, his belt weighed down with an array of daggers and knives.

But he was no match for my black wing. Where the stranger had speed and bursts of rabid energy, Nkita was collected, precise. He was perfection. Every vein pulsed with intensity, every tendon stretched with effort. I knew his heartbeat slowed in his chest as he concentrated because I could feel his pulse in my own wrist, my neck. As mine raced ahead, his held back. When he struck, it mattered. And with a more muscular physique than the red wing, when he struck...it hurt.

"Yield," Nkita said after a time of dueling, both Crylia dripping in sweat.

"Never heard of the word!" the red wing screeched, taking a running leap, spreading his wings, and coming down fierce, sword poised at Nkita's head.

But Nkita dodged his blade, letting his true form show for only a moment. Fur scrawled up his arms and chest and neck, spiraling in striations as his talons showed themselves. The lion and the eagle were one, standing in the form of a two-legged Crylia monster.

Nkita brought his hand against the abdomen of the red wing and turned him, slamming him through the wall of the cabin so that his body sank into the snow outside.

Nkita roared, sword tight in his other fist, and ran through the gap he'd made in the wall, ready to strike. Ready to kill.

But he stopped cold, sword overheard. For the red wing was...*giggling*?

Nkita growled and lowered his sword. "You cannot be so much of an idiot. It's not possible."

The giggling only grew until the red wing popped his head up from the snow like a bunny sniffing out clovers, his sharp nose wrinkled with amusement.

"I could have *killed* you, fool!" Nkita cried.

The red wing pulled himself up, his smile wide and his teeth sharp. His eyes gleamed silver, irises and pupils still mere slivers as though his Crylsight could not leave him even if it wanted to.

"You came to visit me and brought me a present, Nk? I smell something *pretty*," the red wing said, swiping his long tongue over his lips.

"I will warn you once and only once." Nkita pointed his sword at the Cryl. "No."

The red wing waggled his eyebrows. "Ohhh, forbidden fruit, eh? All the better."

"*Dagon.*"

He raised his hands in mock surrender. "Alright, alright. Not forbidden fruit. Just forbidden."

Nkita and the red wing reentered the cabin, stepping over the mess they'd created with their fighting—splintered wood and smashed chairs, torn curtains and groaning walls.

"You can come out, Em," Nkita called.

I stood slowly, smoothing down my hair and tugging at the hem of Nkita's shirt, willing it to cover more of my thighs than it did.

Nkita clearly had forgotten I was not properly dressed, for his entire face changed when he saw me blushing.

"Oh." The red wing devoured me with his eyes, once, twice, three times. "Hello, beautiful. And she's a gold wing! How delicious...."

Nkita aimed the tip of his sword to the hollow beneath the red wing's jaw. "Try that again."

Dagon cleared his throat. "Good evening, most respected young gold wing, friend of the Teth—"

"*Mate*," Nkita corrected.

Dagon's mouth flopped open. "You *married*? You—?"

"*Grand* Teth," I spoke up, crossing my arms. "He's not a Teth anymore than I am a friend." Though the reason for him becoming the Cza's Grand Teth was terrible, Nkita had earned his rank. And this red wing needed to know it.

Dagon grinned all the harder. "Forgive me. Greetings gold wing, *mate* of Grand Teth Nkita Opas, Teth-wed female who I will not touch under *any* circumstances."

Then, he whispered, "Unless she simply *must* have me, we—"

Nkita rammed the hilt of his sword into Dagon's belly so that the red wing doubled over. Then he nodded to me. "Em, this is Dagon Red Wing. He's not to be trusted."

"I see that," I replied. I nodded to the recovering Dagon. "Thank you for letting us use your cabin, Dagon Red Wing who I cannot trust."

Hands on his knees, Dagon let his tongue flop out for a moment. "I like your *dress*."

I narrowed my eyes. "I like your *wall*."

Dagon laughed out in a loud bark. "Now, on to business. You should hide your face if you don't like the sight of blood, Teth-wed. Once the great General helps me put my wall back up, he'll have to help me torture these miscreants I've brought with me. I have a job to do, believe it or not. And if you and your General want to stay...he'll help me do it."

I swallowed. "Torture?"

Dagon's eyes blazed, peril shining in them like silver fire. "Mmm...*torture*."

20

THE DAY THE CRYL WAS TORTURED

"Must we?" I asked Nkita. My fingernails sliced into my palms as I paced through the cabin. "Surely, we can simply...leave?"

"It will not take long," Nkita said. "And you do not have to partake. Just...take a walk or something. I will come find you when we're through."

"So you want me to walk around in nothing but your shirt until you are finished murdering someone?"

"Mhmm."

"Nkita—"

"Well, it's torture. Not necessarily murder, but it usually ends with that outcome, I'm afraid. But what did you think being a General was like, Em? Vecherin? Dancing and wine?"

I crossed my arms. "Is this person Tru? Because if you think I will allow—"

"You know I can't harm your people any longer, Em. If the prisoner is Tru, it will be Dagon who meets his end. Now, would you just trust me and let me do this favor for the red wing?"

I sighed. "I need boots and a coat. At least."

Nkita nodded. "Hold tight."

There was a scuffle, resulting in a string of Crylia swears and a set of snarls. But Nkita returned with Dagon's coat and his boots.

"They won't fit but they'll do for a time. Just put a little distance between you and the cabin. Go until you can no longer hear the screams."

I blinked at my mate. *Oh, he is not making a joke.* I shrugged on the red wing's brown coat and shoved my feet into his enormous boots, turning my ankles to see them better. "There are numerous blades attached to this footwear."

"Yes. Dag is mad but he is resourceful." Nkita pointed at me as he delivered the last of his directions before I departed. "If you need me...just need me."

I pretended to be upset, though his words brought warmth to my cheeks. "I'll be sure not to, General, as you'll be rather busy."

I trudged out of the cabin, passing a scowling Dag in the snow with no boots on, and slipped behind the trees. I thought about going off to find Drosya, but since I did not even know which town we'd lost each other outside of, I decided against it. Instead, I circled right back around until I crouched outside the patched wall of Dagon's cabin. I pulled his coat tight around me and peeked through one of the many holes made by the Crylia brawl that had taken place not an hour before.

There. That is who they are—Good Gua! Oh!

Dagon pinned down the legs, and Nkita took his talons to the chest of the torture victim. He counted out ribs before plunging those talons into the already bleeding flesh of the white wing. The Cryl writhed as he suffered, a steam gurgling in the back of his throat, his wings fullspread but crushed down into the wood of the cabin floor.

I...I know that Cryl. I gasped as I stared, my fingers gripping the jagged opening in the wall. *I know him.*

It was, without a doubt, the white wing who had come to Urol's tavern in Yogdn. The one who was after Letti. The white wing who might remember the face of a tavern maid who'd escaped in the arms of that same Letti.

"Tell us," Nkita said calmly. "What business do you have in Fyerdn?"

Ah. So are were no longer in Led. We'd crossed over into a nearby region, just as I'd thought. But I knew the business the white wing had in Fyerdn. He wanted to find a Tonguekeeper. Only I still had no idea what that was or why he wanted it so badly. It had something to do with Letti. That much was certain.

When the white wing would not answer, Nkita sighed, wiping his bloody hand off on his trousers as though it were a day of chopping wood or mending a wagon wheel. "Break his wing, Dag," he said.

"With unmatchable pleasure," Dagon replied.

A loud, heart-chilling crunch and more screams than I could endure. But Nkita did not so much as twitch in response. Dagon, on the other hand, grinned, his tongue lopping out.

"Again," Nkita said. "Why are you in Fyerdn?"

"I don't know!" the white wing bellowed.

"You *don't know* why you're in Fyerdn?" Nkita nodded to Dag. "Get the other wing."

"Wait!" I cried out. Then I clamped my hand over my mouth. *Emyri, why?!* I swiveled, rushing away from the cabin and losing a boot in the process.

Dagon raced out of the cabin, taking flight and landing before me, his wings spread in the falling snow. "Seems we are torturing the wrong Crylia," he said, wrinkling his nose. "Unless the little Grounded wants to tell us what she knows about this white wing."

"Stay away from me," I said, curling my fingers around the blade at the ankle of the boot I'd borrowed from the Cryl who threatened me.

"Oh, I won't hurt you," Dag said, tilting his head, his eyes wild. "Not now. Not in front of Nk." He nodded his head toward the cabin. "I'd have to get rid of him first. And if you don't want that...better start talking, beautiful."

Nkita leaned out of the cabin door. "Are you needing me, Em?" he asked coolly.

I stood up and turned my back on Dagon. "Yes. I must...speak with you. Just with you."

Dagon motioned forward. "Please. Use my cabin. Take your time." He smiled, his teeth sharp, his eyes cutting through the gray haze of the storm.

I rescued my snow-sunken boot and walked as calmly as I could to my mate. Once we were inside, I tried to ignore the whimpering, trembling Crylia that was tied to the table.

"Careful," Nkita said, scooting me over so I did not step in the pooling blood. "Now...do you truly know something, Em?"

I didn't need to answer that. When the white wing realized it was me, he lunged forward, despite his injuries, dragging the table with him. "You! It's *you!*" he hacked, blood spewing from between his shattered teeth.

"Emyri," Nkita said, blocking the white wing from my view and looking into my eyes. "What did you *do?*"

111

21

The Day The Red Wing Bargained

"Must you assume I've done something—"

"I know you did something, Emyri. You reek of secrecy. And you have since the moment I found you in Ydr. Out with it. What did you do to get yourself embroiled with such a white wing? Do you even know who this is? What he does?"

Ydr. That is the name of the town where he found me and that's where Drosya will be. I tucked that information away for the moment I could use it. "I only know that this white wing came into a tavern where I worked when I"—I swallowed.

"When you left me, forsaking our vows?"

I squinted at my mate. "Those could hardly pass for vows, Nkita."

"Finish telling me your partial truth, Em. This Cryl is bleeding out, and I haven't got all day."

I sighed, loosening my shoulders as the white wing lunged for me once more, struggling against the weight of the table in his increasingly weakened state. "He had two other white wings with him. They were looking for someone. Or at least that's what the gossip led me to believe."

"What sort of someone?"

I shrugged.

"Emyri, must I press you?"

"Fine. A...Tonguekeeper. But I don't know—"

Without another second of hesitation, Nkita drew his sword, flourished it and swung it down swiftly, taking the white wing's head.

I shrieked, backing away from the entire ordeal as blood came rushing for me once more. I scrubbed at the crimson splatters on my neck and arms, trying to remember that breathing was important for my survival.

"I should have warned you, I suppose," Nkita growled.

"Y-you suppose?! Nkita...what...why?"

"Speak nothing more of this," he said. "Let's go."

I shook my head. "Go? But I thought—"

"Now, Em. I will explain later."

"No." I reclaimed my arm when he tried to take hold of my elbow. "You will explain now. I am not to be dragged about, following your orders, Nkita. You are not my General. You are my *mate*."

"Which means something very different to you than it does to me."

"I don't care what it means to either of us. I care about how you treat me. Keep your sentimentalities and your customs and perceptions. I care about your actions. And I insist—no, I demand—that you treat me like I am at least partially capable of my own self-preservation."

He glared at me. "So...you prefer to risk your life by chatting here in this cabin?"

"Inform me, so I can make my own decisions."

Nkita wiped the white wing's blood off his blade. If he weren't in black, I would have seen the crimson smear against his trousers. "The Czas have been hunting for Tonguekeepers for generations. And if the Cza finds one, or anyone who knows where one is, he will extract every fraction of dignity from that person through every agony-inflicting technique his Zyeza can come up with."

I shivered. "Zyeza...?"

"An elite pedigree of black wings tethered to the Cza for the sole purpose of torturing until dead. Brother clan to the Hresh, white wings skilled in the art of tracking down and retrieving targets, no matter how hidden." I glanced at the rather dead white wing on the cabin floor. There had been three of them. Three Hresh. That meant there were at least two more on the hunt.

I nodded. "So if I were to have knowledge of the whereabouts of someone suspected to have knowledge of the whereabouts of a Tonguekeeper...?"

"We need to run. Harder. Faster. Now."

My eyes followed Nkita's as they darted to the door. Dagon was outside. And he'd been bent on finding out what the white wing knew. Somehow, our host was involved. I held out my hand to Nkita. "I see."

"Stubborn."

"Demanding."

"Can we stop arguing and go, woman?"

We took the back door, tiptoeing as we hastened. But as soon as our boots hit the ground, we heard a flurry of wings. Dagon landed before us, barefoot in the snow.

"Where are we headed?" he asked.

"Off to pick berries," I responded without thinking.

"In a snowstorm?"

"Galeberries. Have you never heard of them?"

Dagon sniffed the air between us, oblivious to the icy torrent blasting against the side of his face. "I'm not a berry Cryl," he explained. "Prefer my meat still wriggling."

"Let me bake you a galeberry pie, and I promise I will change your mind."

Dagon chuckled, his temperature so well adjusted that he burned puddles into the drifts where he stood. "Here's what we will do. You spend the night in my cabin, the both of you. And you tell me all about the Tongue-keeper I'm looking for. After that, you can lie still, and he can have his way with you. Then...off you go. You can pick as many berries as you want, and I will go after my meat."

"Or...we leave—" Nkita began.

"We'll stay," I answered, cutting off my mate.

"We most certainly will not—"

"But only if you tell us what you know, Dagon. An even trade of information. A truth for a truth."

Dagon grinned, his gaze flirting with Nkita. "She's a different sort." He stuck his tongue out. "Has you by the downfeathers, doesn't she?"

Nkita only responded by putting his hand on my waist as we walked back to the cabin.

"Don't be mad," I whispered.

"And you accuse me of doing whatever I want and expecting you to follow."

"It's just one night."

"Night belongs to two alone—the killers and the killed, Em. Didn't your teachers ever school you properly?"

"I want the information. It's priceless."

"Better prepare then, Grounded."

I bit my lip, surprised to find I still wore no ring. Even more surprised by how much it hurt for Nkita to call me that. "Prepare?"

"To decide which you are." He held my hand as I entered the cabin yet again. "Killer. Or the Killed."

22

THE DAY THE BLADE SANK DEEP

Dagon stirred the pot, a strange and bitter scent filling the cabin. *At least it's warm, despite the odor.*

Nkita growled, his back against the wall and his legs stretched out as he reclined on the floor. "How long will you be minding the food, Dagon? You're not a kitchen maid. On with this."

Dagon hissed at Nkita, still stirring. "Artistry cannot be rushed, black wing. You rushed yours, and look at the results. My only lead is headless!" Dagon motioned to the Hresh white wing that no one had bothered to pile into the corner or toss out of doors. His stiffening body was still fastened to the table. I had never been more grateful to be permitted a seat on the floor instead of a chair.

"I did not rush my artistry, Dag," Nkita said, crossing his arms. "And your gruel is not art."

Dag scooped the stew into two bowls and hopped over the dead body with a little skip and a grin. He handed one of the bowls to each of us.

"None for you?" I asked, eyeing the food with justifiable suspicion.

"I'll get mine in the hunt," Dag replied, running his long pointed tongue across his teeth. "But I'm not one for poison so...eat." He plopped down on the floor, spreading himself out in a reclined position on his side and propping his head up on one arm. With a twinkle of his fingers, he reached out and pinched the tip of Nkita's boot.

"No." Nkita barked. He took a large bite of stew and grumbled.

I couldn't help but chuckle. "It's that good, is it?"

"It's awful," Nkita said, shoveling three steaming bites into his mouth one after another. With his mouth full, he continued. "I hate it."

The stew was indeed remarkable. The flavors were complex, the textures rich, the rabbit roasted before being simmered for charred, fragrant notes.

"Dagon, you are a marvelous cook!" I confessed.

He flicked his thumb against his nose with pride. "Now...onto the trading of information. I will give my guests the first question."

"Why are you being so nice?" Nkita asked, narrowing his eyes at the red wing.

"That's an odd question to start with. Hm...I suppose it's warm in here, and I am cozy."

"Not buying it."

"Well, I'll keep selling regardless." Dagon pinched my naked foot next. "Lady Nkita...*where* is the Tonguekeeper?"

"Dagon," Nkita warned.

"Might as well cut to it, General. And this is a lot nicer than torture, don't you think?"

I leaned forward and smacked his hand away from my toes. "I don't know who the Tonguekeeper is, largely because I don't know what that is."

Dagon scrunched up his nose. "What unlearned off-shoot of a border town must you have come from to have not heard the legend of the Tonguekeeper?"

"Just tell me. Insulting me won't help you find anything."

Dagon flopped over and lay on his back, spreading his legs and arms wide, his wings tucked behind him. "The Tonguekeeper holds the secrets of Old Cryl. The words that formed the world have an origin. And the Tonguekeeper—"

"Keeps it," I finished for him. "And what do you want this Tonguekeeper for, Dag? To what end?"

"Oh, just...two hundred thousand gold coin, is all."

"Who's the job for, red?" Nkita asked. "Grand Teth Brinbas? I know it's not the Cza. He'd never do dealings with you. Not after the last time."

"Big Cryl who runs for the rebels hired me. Goes by the name Cyndr."

I sat up straight. "I'm sorry...did you just say Cyndr? A...a burly white wing?"

"You know Cyndi? He's a little rough to have befriended a delicate thing like you—"

"What do Cyndr and the rebels want with the Tonguekeeper?"

"Don't know," Dagon said. "Don't care. Truthfully, I want the gold. And Lady Nkita knows where the Tonguekeeper is—"

"I don't know. I...she...." I glanced at Nkita, wondering if I should confess.

To my awe, the Grand Teth spread his arms and beckoned for me to come closer.

Confused, I scooted myself toward him until I leaned against his chest. It reminded me of leaning against him when he'd come back from battle. Of being trapped in the Castle and begging for even one moment together.

"I met her in a tavern in Yogdn."

"Oh. Dreadful town." Dagon clicked his teeth.

"Oh yes, it was horrid. But she was married to a Cryl named Urol. He was...also horrid. But Umra was kind. And one day, three white wings came in looking for a Tonguekeeper. The moment she learned of this, Umra fled and she took me with her. Right out the window. Who knows what the white wings would have done to me if she'd left me behind—"

Dagon sat up. "Where is she now? This Umra?"

"I don't know, but—"

"We can find her mate," Dagon said. "Won't be so hard to bring them together after that."

I shook my head. "No, she...she severed the bond between her and Urol. She even offered to do the same for me"—my words died on my lips, for Nkita's muscles tightened beneath me. "I wouldn't—I would never—"

"No one cares about your fragile, makeshift bond," Dagon said. "Where did she go? Where is she now?"

"She...left."

"She's lying," Nkita said.

I angled so I could look up at him. "Pardon me, General?"

"I know when you're lying, Em. You're lying."

"Ha! Em the liar!" Dagon cried out.

"Oahra," both Nkita and I corrected at once.

"Oh, only he can call you Em, eh? Adorable. So you do know where—"

I curled myself up so I fit perfectly against Nkita. His black wing unfurled, wrapping around my shoulders. "She told me her name was Letti and she took me to the mountains of Led. And left me for...well, I told her my mate would be hunting for me and that his name was...Rizel—"

"What?" Nkita sat up, throwing me off him. "She took you to Rizel?"

"I am alright, obviously—"

"This is getting good," Dag laughed. "That wicked black wing? Oh, he hates you, Nk!"

"He hurt you?" Nkita asked me, ignoring Dagon. Then, he stood up. "I'm going."

I grabbed Nkita's calf and held on. "No, you're not *walking* to Led."

Nkita cursed. Clearly he'd forgotten he could not fly without two wings.

"I handled Rizel," I explained. "And then I met Cyndr—"

"You met—"

Dagon grabbed my abandoned bowl of soup, stood, and smashed it into the floor, sending the contents flying and cracking the bowl to pieces. "*Where is the Tonguekeeper*?!"

Nkita stepped forward, going chest to chest with the red wing. "Mind your manners."

"Enough stalling—"

Nkita must have grabbed a blade from one of Dag's boots because he sank it into the red wings ribs not once, but twice.

Dagon gave a little giggle and grinned at Nkita. "Quick, you black wings," he murmured. Then, he fell to his knees, his hand clutching his wounds as blood bubbled over his fingers.

"You'll be alright," Nkita said, his face unflinching, his voice cool. "Take a rest, friend." And then to me, he offered a hand. "You have your information. And if you don't come with me now, I will be forced to carry you."

"You...*killed*—"

Nkita Opas grabbed Dag's boots and coat, put his arm around my waist, and dragged me out of the cabin.

23

THE DAY THE CRYL CHANGED COURSE

The snow beat against us both until Nkita placed me in front of him, using his wing to shield me from the harsh wind. It would have been romantic if my body hadn't already gone numb.

"We can stop in the nesting grounds up ahead," he said, bending so his frozen lips met my ear. "And hide in the caves along the hills until morning. Dag will not expect me to go there. It is where Cryl go to...."

To lay their eggs. Oh, Gua help the helpless. No wonder Dagon would never think to find Nkita among the nesting fathers. He was not the nurturing sort.

"Nkita!" I had to shout to be heard. "What is a Tonguekeeper?"

"Em, not now! Just walk!"

"What is it, and why is the Cza in need of one?"

"*Emyri Izela.* Not. Now!"

I dug my heels into the snow, forcing us to come to a stop.

Nkita roared with frustration. "Something in your head is *broken*, woman!"

"Tonguekeeper! Explanation! Or you will sink into the snow trying to carry me the rest of the way."

Nkita shouted as he hoisted me out of the snow and then set me back down, pushing us forward. "The world is made of words!"

"What?!"

"It's made of *words*!"

I laughed. He sounded drunk. "The world is made of the *tears of Gua*!"

"Gua isn't real, Em! It's a fantasy that your people made up to feel safe!"

"And you are an *idiot*, Crylia! Why would I *ever* entertain that thought, even for a moment?"

"Because you asked me what a Tonguekeeper is, and I am trying to explain it to you!"

"Fine! Speak! I will just add Gua back into the story myself!"

He grunted. "That is what the world is made of. Words. *Old* words. The Tonguekeeper stores the knowledge of those words! She is very powerful. She can change things."

"You sound...so stupid, Nkita."

"Excuse me?!"

"If the world is made of words and there is no Gua...who spoke the first ones?"

Nkita slipped on a patch of ice, nearly taking us down. But I held him up with a strained groan of my own. *He is as heavy as he is stubborn.*

"The words weren't spoken, foolish human! They just...were."

"*How*?!"

"I don't *know*! I wasn't there! The first person who was there...*they* were the Tonguekeeper. And when they die, a new Tonguekeeper is chosen to receive their knowledge. Now let us move before we freeze!"

"So...the Cza...he wants to force them to change something? To use their Old words?"

"I don't know. I'm not the Cza, either! Now, if you don't hasten your sluggish steps, we will be buried alive in the snow!"

"Letti. She used words!"

Nkita's rage died down. "She...she did?"

"She could carry me long distances after she uttered words. And make me fall asleep. And she claimed she could sever our bond with words as well."

"You...you truly met the Tonguekeeper then?"

"I...think so. But she traded me to Rizel. There was something she wanted. Something he had."

"What would a Tonguekeeper ever have need of? This makes no sense!"

"We will have to figure it out."

"Em! *We* are not figuring this out—"

"Nkita! It's my job!"

125

A wave of heat left the Cryl's body in a blast, forcing me to step away from him in the deep snow. "You're still trying to *spy for the Tru*?!"

I screamed so loudly that my throat went raw. "I don't have a *choice*!"

The General began to march forward, and I knew I had to keep up with him if I wanted to survive the night. But we'd changed course, Nkita taking a sharp left.

"Where are we going?" I asked, panting from the effort it took to catch up to him. "Nkita?"

"To find the truth you're hiding from me!"

I gripped his arm, my fingernails sinking into his skin. *If only he were not made of muscle and pride, I could steer him away from his new intentions.* But no, the Cryl was more stubborn than I ever would be.

"We are going to the nesting grounds to—"

He turned on me once more. "If you don't tell me why you spy for the Tru like your life depends on it, I will find out why myself. You have three seconds, *mate*. Three...."

"Nkita, please. I am going to freeze to death out here—"

"Two...."

"And a warm bed, just the two of us, we could be *together*—"

He did not bother counting to one. He continued marching to what I knew in my heart was the east. But if Nkita crossed into the land of the Tru tribes, I would not be able to follow. If they caught him, I would not be able to rescue him. And if he found out my secret... I would not be able to look him in the eye ever again.

24

THE DAY THE ARROWS FLEW

"Slow down," I said, falling behind as Nkita pushed forward. The rising sun began to melt the snow that had assailed us all night long. I trudged waist deep, my limbs numb and my body refusing to follow my orders.

"If you are tired, I can carry you," he grumbled.

I didn't want Nkita to carry me. I wanted him to turn around. And if I couldn't get my way on that, maybe I could slow him down. Stall him.

"Nkita, be reasonable."

"I am the most reasonable Cryl you've ever met."

"No. You are wildly stubborn and unrelenting. A reasonable Cryl would never have chosen me as his mate in the first place."

We were nearing the border. I felt Gua's waters rushing under frozen rivers nearby. Home. It was so near but it remained unattainable.

"I know, Em."

I stopped to rest my legs, climbing up on a boulder so I could rub them back to life. "You know?"

"I know what it is like to be tethered."

"I am no Teth, Nkita," I scoffed.

He turned around, coming back to me so he could rub his warm hands on my calves. "I know what it's like to be assigned to a mission against your will. To be forced to serve something you don't love. Something you fear. I cannot break that tether for me. But if I can break whatever enslaves you, I will."

"Nkita."

He put his hand on my neck. "Em. What happened?"

I shook my head. "I am too cold to think."

He climbed atop the boulder and sat down beside me. "Come here."

"How—?"

But I had no time to think of how I might maneuver myself. Nkita reached out, taking my rear in his hands and turning me so that I faced him, my legs straddling him, my calves scraping against the rough surface of the stone. In moments, the ice crystals on that boulder melted away from the General's heat. Crylia were magnificent creatures when they weren't warring against humans and mounting our heads on spikes.

"Closer," he said, his words tickling my jaw.

"Oh?" I slid my frozen hands over his shoulders. "You forgive me now?"

"Absolutely never."

I frowned. "If you're just going to torture me again, I would rather die in the snow."

He kissed my neck, his teeth sinking into my skin when he reached my shoulder. "You'll take what you get."

Oh, he makes me so furious. I wanted to march off just to show him I didn't care. That I didn't want him. That his body and his attention did not matter to me. But...my legs were already parted. And he was already inside me.

I gasped at the heat of him as I rocked, as his fingers slid up my shirt and dug into the skin of my back. Briefly, I remembered how we consummated our marriage. How the Teth were made to watch as the Cza presided over us. How still I was made to lay and how Nkita sought to cover me with his wings, all the while knowing that he was the Pureblood Heir, that the Cza would make him pay and use me to do it.

But no one is watching us now.

So I put my lips on his, sighing into the warmth of his mouth. I told myself to relax, to let the cold and the fear leave my body for once. And I told myself this over and over until my muscles released their tension. The moment I let go, Nkita knew. It was as if we were connected. As if he could feel me inside him, almost as truly as I felt him inside me.

This frightened me all over again. And my muscles began to tighten.

"No," he mumbled against my mouth, squeezing the back of my neck. "Don't go."

I bit his lip in my effort to calm myself again, but it was all no use. I wasn't ready for what he had in store for me, and it was my own damn fault.

Nkita cursed as he finished without me, pulling back just enough to look me in the eyes. "Em...."

I shook my head, still breathless. "I'm...sorry—"

"Don't apologize. Not for that." It would always surprise me when he was gentle. When the hands that had killed hundreds of my people touched my face with affection. "Let's get you someplace warm."

Perfect. I nodded. "Like the nesting grounds?"

"More like...a Tru village."

"Nkita!"

Just then, Nkita's breath caught. "Stay," he whispered, barely audible. "We are surrounded, it seems."

Surrounded? I held tight to Nkita, panic swelling in my heart. "The Hresh, come to take you to the Cza?"

Nkita plucked my lips with his. One last kiss. "No. Not Cryl this time."

That is when I understood. We were surrounded not by Crylia come to take Nkita to the Cza, but by humans, come to kill Nkita where he sat. They waited only for the right moment to send a spear through the heart of the monster I loved. And when it came to the Crylia, they would have no mercy. They would make sure he died in the forest, his blood spilling on the boulder where I'd failed to yield to him.

If he could fly, we'd escape. If he could fight, we would win. But he could not fly because his wing was gone. And he could not fight because he was bonded to my people, just as he was bonded to me.

"It's alright," he said to me, his dark eyes on mine.

"I...." I swallowed, trying to keep my hands from shaking. "I will buy you time, Nkita Opas. And you must escape. Promise me."

"I will never agree—"

The arrows flew like falcons aimed at their prey. Two into the back of my black wing Crylia and one into my hip. I would have fallen backward into the snow if Nkita hadn't locked onto me, wrapping his hand around my forearm and holding fast.

As soon as I could force myself upward, and before the next round of arrows could flow from the Tru bows, I stood on that boulder and lifted a hand into the air.

"The dead call to the dead!" I screamed at the top of my lungs, leaving Cryl behind and speaking in Tru. "And the living cannot answer!"

I tarried, blood rushing down my thigh as I waited to see whether the Tru would obey their own laws and take me in for my death sentencing. Or whether they would take my life in the forest, no water to claim my soul.

25

THE DAY THE COMMANDER APPEARED

One can never know that they are looking at the Tru.

We move like water gliding down the veins of a leaf. Like sun spilling over the treeline at dawn. Where the Crylia stand erect, their wings regal and intimidating, casting shadows on all beneath...the Tru shift as subtle as shadows.

There was one of them, though, who stepped forward with her chin lowered, her cyan eyes burning through me. She was Tru-hana, her blue markings evident through the flow of her bone-straight hair, the tips of her fingers and nose. Even in the cold, she wore little clothing, her bare feet proud as she balanced atop the snow.

"The traitor returns for her sentencing," she said, her words full and low and round as she spoke in my native tongue.

She could not know, of course, how the sound of her voice made me want to weep, made me want to curl up before a fire and fall asleep listening to stories of Gua. It had been so long since I'd heard the tones of the Tru, the lushness of the voice of my people.

"Keep trained on her," the warrior instructed her soldiers. "And kill the monster—"

"He's my *mate*." I spoke the words as quickly as I could, my hands shaking, one arm still in the air.

The warrior stopped, pain and anger seething through her gaze. The white paint on her forehead and cheeks were to help her blend with the snow, but she stood out to me like a flame in the dead of night. It had been so long...so long.

"Then he will endure the same fate as you. And I assure you...your fate will not be kind, Emyri Izela—"

"*Izzy!*" a voice interrupted. "Move! Get out of my way!"

A sob humbled me. I collapsed, my legs folding beneath me as another Tru-ori parted through the warriors and ran to me. She wrapped me in her arms, weeping into my hair.

"You came *home!*" she said, her tears warming me as they fell.

"Cevae," I gasped. "We can't...."

"I *don't care!*" She sat me down, scrubbing at her leaking nose as she surveyed my leg, her golden features glowing in the early morning light. She turned her head, just for a moment. "What is *wrong with you*, Yahara?!" she scolded the blue-haired commander. "You would let her bleed out like this?"

To me she nodded. "Hold still." And she wiped at her face, sniffling. "I-it is difficult for me to see th-through the tears."

Then, she cracked the arrow in half, pressing my wound with one gloved hand, putting her free hand on my cheek as I groaned. "I'm sorry, I know."

I took her hand in mine and kissed it, my own tears carving their paths down my cheeks. "Cevae...."

A soft curse from Yahara. "The monster is gone. Perfect. The traitor was just distracting us."

Perfect indeed. With Nkita gone, I could pray to Gua for his safety. Perhaps he would find the rebels and fight for his right to the throne of Crylia. Perhaps he would become the Cza our people needed.

Or maybe he would find the Tonguekeeper and sever our bond, once and for all. For all that it would break my heart, I would be relieved for him to be free of me.

"We must carry her," Cevae said, her golden waves fluttering around my shoulders as she leaned her forehead against mine. "She's not even dressed for this weather, Yahara."

"She is Tru. She should be acclimated—"

"Well, she is not!" Cevae raised her voice at her cousin, her chest heaving, her hands still holding mine. I had never heard her speak with such authority, and especially not to our commander. Or rather, to her commander. I did not belong to my tribe any longer.

Yahara's eyes flashed blue, lightning against a stormy sky. "She can walk."

"Yayo—"

"She. Can. *Walk*."

Cevae straightened her shoulders. "Then I will walk beside—"

"You will take the lead, Tomora Cevae. Now."

When Cevae would not release me, I nodded my head and squeezed her hands. "Go, Vae."

It hurt. When she let go of my hands. When she crossed the clearing and took the lead of the troops, heading us deeper into Tru territory.

Yahara approached, gripping my upper arm and yanking me to my feet. "I will watch you myself. The slippery ones like to try to get away, and by Gua, you will be tried this time."

"I...can barely move," I confessed, limping along, my legs already frozen, my body losing energy with each moment.

"Don't worry. I will not let you have the honor of dying here in Gua's precious snow. You will go on dry land, in flames. In shame. And I will watch as justice is served and feel no pain."

"Yahara—"

"Say my name again. Let my name leave your mouth and see what happens to you."

I struggled, doing my best to keep my legs moving through the waist-deep snow until I could go no further.

136

Until the darkness fell over my eyes and my limbs shuddered to sleep. My only comforts were that Nkita had gone and that I would meet my end in the arms of Gua after all.

26

THE DAY THE TRU-HANA SPOKE

Sweetwood burning on a fire brought me back. *Is this...is this a blanket?* I reached to my torso to explore the soft fabric draped over me, but found my wrists were bound.

A pang of sorrow echoed through my body. *I am not free here. I am not free anywhere. Not anymore.*

I was able to sit up, though the pain in my leg from the arrow was determined to make movement difficult. My back was against warm brick. Whichever home I was being kept in, I knew the bricks were baked one at a time in the sun during warm weather and laid by hand. Some- one loved this home. The Tru built all things that way, from homes to trades to relationships. One at a time. By hand. On purpose.

Someone had bathed me and placed me in a clean dress, the wool warm and welcomed. I felt at ease as I looked around.

The home was one room. A cauldron bubbled over the hearth, and the door swung open loosely, creaking in the chilled breeze. The heavy winter curtains in the glassless windows were weaved, stitch by stitch, and by the look of it, the weaver was very talented. *Perhaps an elder's home, then. Or at least someone with weaving talent.*

"Ah. You are awake. I knew sleep wouldn't keep you for long."

Gua help the helpless. Oh no. I bit my cheek to keep myself from saying these things out loud. The man was tall, with a physique carved from years of climbing mountains and deep diving in the western seas. His Tru-hana markings meant his hair was bathed in a brilliant blue and braided long down his back, the sides of his head shaved into patterns to tell the story of his conquests.

He kept his topaz eyes trained on me, his posture still. *Where...is his shirt? It is freezing outside. And how did he manage to work up a sweat?*

"I came in for this," he said, nearly reading my mind as he grabbed a hand-knit woolen shirt from a hook by the door and pulled it on over his head, revealing a frustrating rippling of abdominal muscles. "And to check on you, of course." He cleared his throat, fiddling with his neck and the beaded bands he wore around it. "The water suits you, Izela."

Why...is he being kind? He should be worse to me than Yahara. He should refuse to see me. Or...try to strangle me. Something more than pleasantries.

I cracked my mouth open, my words croaking out of me. "The rivers are yours, Mahopi."

He didn't smile when I returned his blessing. Instead, he sighed. "What are you doing here?"

"I...didn't mean to be here. It just happened."

"It just happened? You forgot where the borders are, Iz? You simply stumbled onto Tru land? And with...with a Cryl?"

"So much has happened—"

"*Nothing* has happened." There it was. The anger I knew Maho was hiding. "Nothing has happened since you left. Everyone is just...waiting. And broken. And breaking. I—"

"I'm sorry, Maho."

"No. You're not."

I *was* sorry. Sorry that I missed my family. That I did not turn out the way that any of them would have wanted. That I could not be with my unit or my friends or my people ever again. That I would be killed for my mistakes. But he was right. I could not actually be sorry for what I did.

"When...when do you think the execution—?"

"I am not going to let them *hurt you*, Iz. You must know at least that much."

"Maho...if you intervene—"

He laughed. A bitter thing. And leaned a capable arm against the door frame. "As usual. You haven't listened to a word I've said. There are no stakes left for me. For

140

any of us. We won't let anyone take you away. Never again. That's a promise."

"Yahara—"

"Yahara makes herself seem strong and important and fierce. But she has cried every day since you left, Iz."

My eyes burned with tears of my own, my throat swelling with emotion. "I'm sorry—"

"*Who is he*?"

"W-what?"

"Don't. You *know* that I know what you're good at. You *know* that I know you can lie. Well. And pretend to be innocent. And ignorant. But I know that *you know* I am perceptive as well, Iz. And everyone in this unit is leaving out details about this Cryl and how you were found and what he was doing to you. So...are you going to tell me, or am I going to come to my own conclusions?"

I took a deep breath. "Maho—"

"*Cryl be damned*, Iz! That's what you've been busy doing in Crylia? Spreading your legs?"

Tears threatened to burst free, but I refused to let them fall. "I am a *spy*, Maho. Perhaps you thought that job would be easy—"

He left, slamming the door behind him so hard that the home shook.

I leaned my head back on the wall and wished I could go back to sleep. Or at least free my hands and run. But the door creaked open, and a sweet, golden-haired Tru slipped in.

"Cevae...."

She raced across the room and threw her arms around me. Then, she kissed my face a dozen times.

I did cry then. I couldn't help it.

She caught my tears with her sleeve, and if my hands were free, I would have caught hers.

"I'm so happy to see you, Izzy," she squeaked. "Really. I prayed and prayed that you would come home."

"So you're the one who did this to me, eh?"

She laughed, curling up on the bed beside me. "Tell me everything."

"Oh, that's not a very good idea, Vae."

"Tell me...something, then. Anything."

I leaned my chin on the top of her head. "Mmm...I have...been all over Crylia, now. Well, a lot of it, at least."

"Really? I imagined you would be stationed in one place."

"That was the plan. But that is not how it went." I thought for a moment. "I met some awful, horrible Cryl. And some kind ones too."

She sat up. "*Kind* Cryl?"

"I owe many my life at this point."

"Have you met all the different kinds of them? I heard white is the most terrible."

I grinned. "White wings are mostly all show, if you ask me. They are the most pretentious but they love power, for the most part. Gray wings are the most gentle but can also be the most spiteful. Red wings are...." I thought of Dagon with a chuckle. "Red wings are insane, which makes them strangely entertaining. They also have good taste in boots. And blades. I haven't met any silver. Or any other gold wings—"

"Other?"

Oh. I am not pretending to be Cryl. I forgot. "But I met plenty of Grounded." Out of habit, I licked my lip, feeling for my ring. It was still missing.

"And...." Vae whispered the next part. "And *black wings*?"

"White wings love power, yes? They crave it, they seek it. But black wings...already have it. They *are* power."

"They still scare me." She shivered.

"Me too, if I'm honest."

"Did you meet any Generals, Iz?"

I nodded my head. "Sure did."

Iz smoothed her hand over my hair. She must have been the one to untangle it for me while I slept. "I saw what that black wing was doing to you in the forest."

"It's...it's part of my job, Vae. Don't be sad about that." *Oh, what a lying liar I am.*

"It's not fair that you had to do that."

I met her eyes. "Yes. It is."

She sighed. "Everyone is so emotional now that you're back. Especially Yahara. And even more especially, Mahopi. He spoke with you?"

"He did. For a bit."

"Was he unkind?"

"He was much nicer than I thought he would be."

Vae gave a little smile. "He has been practicing forgiving you. In case you ever came back to him."

"That can never—"

"He was to be your mate, Izzy. You can't fault him for holding onto hope. He's still wildly in love with you."

Oh. I am taken. Very, very taken. I squirmed against the ropes around my wrists. "Do you know when the execution might be planned, Vae?"

"That's not going to happen. Your unit will protect you."

"Yahara—"

"Won't let them. Angry as she is. She will fight, Izzy."

That's what Maho said. "I am not going to allow any of you to get hurt on my behalf. I did what I did, and I was granted leniency. I violated that agreement and now I will pay."

Cevae's gaze lit, as though a fire blazed to life behind her eyes. "No."

"*No?*"

"You did what you thought was right, and we all know it."

I swallowed, my mouth suddenly dry. "It was treason, Tomora Cevae. *High* treason."

"And we're your unit. We're your family." She huffed. "When we were cobbled together and tasked to fight battles on behalf of the Tru...Yahara was a mother. Mahopi was a fisherman. I was a weaver and a child. You were a storyteller, Izela. Beni, a horseman. Shava, a brick layer. We did not know how to fight. Or how to spy. Or how to survive in the wilderness, Cryl breathing down our necks. But we lived because we had one another." She took a big breath. "Yahara is our commander, Iz. But we lived because we had *you*."

"I'm just a storyteller, Vae. Like you said."

"You were our *courage*." She began to untie my hands. "These bindings are foolish. You would never—"

"Tomora Cevae." We both gasped as Yahara appeared in the doorway. "I need time with the prisoner."

"But—"

"Now."

27

THE DAY THE HERBS STUNG

Yahara refastened the ropes around my wrists and pulled them tighter than they needed to be, tugging until I winced.

"You're angry with me—"

"Shut up."

"Yayo—"

She slapped me. Quite decently. What she didn't expect was for a whimper to leave me when she did it.

Her glare softened in an instant, and she took my face in her hands, careful blue eyes studying me. "I hurt you."

"I'm fine," I mumbled. "Sore from...earlier." From Urol, from Rizel, from Cyndr. From every day since I left Tru. Except for when I was with Nkita. That was... a different type of sore.

With quick fingers, she untied the ropes. Then she began her examination, her hands testing my arms, my calves.

"Someone has already cared for me." When she ignored my remark, I tried again. "Yahara—"

"Shut up! Shut up, shut up!"

I stopped her, taking her hands in my own. "You are supposed to be tough and mean, remember? You're the commander."

"Well, you're my sister, fool. And I thought you were *dead*. And then I saw you with that Cryl and I thought you were worse than dead. He...he hurt you, and I was—"

"No. Yahara, listen—"

"What were you *thinking*, Izela? Going off and—what were you thinking? My entire life is ruined because *your* entire life is ruined. I don't know how to separate you from me! None of us do!"

"I'm *sorry*."

"No, you're not! And maybe Vae thinks you are. Or Maho, but—"

"Maho is just as angry with me as you are."

"Well, he expected you to run into his arms, Iz!"

"I *can't*!"

"Why not?!"

"First of all, I was tied to a bed. So no running anywhere. Second of all...hiding me here is incriminating all of you. There is only one option that keeps you safe. Turn me in. If you let me go, they will find out you had me and—"

Yahara slapped me again. But this time, my hands were free. I leaped forward, ignoring the pain in my body, and wrestled her to the ground. She shoved me, and I punched her. She kneed me, and I scratched her face.

When we were both exhausted, we crawled away from each other, panting.

"I *hate you*," Yahara said, her tears slipping down her nose and cheeks, her azure hair in chaos.

"How are the kids?"

She sniffled. "...Good. Ielo is so big." She motioned to her collarbone. "About so tall, last time I was permitted leave to see them."

"Causing you trouble?"

She chuckled. "Most of the letters from home are Duna telling me he doesn't know what to do with him."

The longing to see my nephew ached through my soul. "You have to turn me in, Yahara."

"I can't."

"You have to."

"None of us can go through this again—"

"He's my *mate*." I blurted it out and closed my eyes for a moment, waiting.

"Who?"

"The black wing."

"What...?"

"General Nkita Opas—"

"Stop."

"He's my mate."

"He forced you to—"

"No." I sniffled as I inhaled, my heart pulverizing my ribs. "No, I'm in love with him."

Yahara laughed. Then she laughed more. So much that she had to tip her head back to let it all out. When she was finished, she caught her breath. "You're lying. I know you've always been good at that, but you have increased in your talents of deception, Iz. Well done."

"We're married."

"Was it under duress?"

"Yes."

"Then it doesn't count, now does it?"

"I would have done it anyway."

"Doesn't matter. He's *no one* as far as I am concerned. Worse than that. He is my enemy."

"He's my mate, Yahara."

"He's no brother of mine. If I see him, I will kill him. Easy. A dozen arrows to the heart."

"I didn't tell you this to make you more angry. I told you because...Ya, he will come for me. I don't want you getting hurt."

"If only Oma and Opa lived to see this absolute *shite*."

"You're not listening—"

"Oh, I heard you. I heard you. You are telling me that I should turn you into the Queen to be executed for your crimes. And with haste. Not because you are guilty. Or because you deserve death—which you *do*—but because your death-mongering, child-murdering Crylia lover is coming to shove his member in you again, and we all had better not get in his way. Did I get all that?"

"Please. You don't understand—"

"Mahopi!" She stood up. "Mahopi, get in here!"

"No! Yahara, I told you in confidence!"

"Confidence? You told me out of *spite*!"

"When have I ever been spiteful towards you? Please...."

She frowned, her pretty face contorted into a scowl that held years of betrayal, loss, and pain.

"What is wrong?" Maho asked, sticking his head through the open window, shoving the curtain aside and letting in a blast of cold air.

"We...." Yahara began.

"You are taking me to the Queen," I finished for my sister. "Yahara is loyal to Her Goodness. I...I will not object."

Maho shook his head. "I'm not doing that."

"Maho—"

"We will all finish our day. And then get some sleep," Yahara said. "Tomorrow, we will make our decisions. Gua will be patient with us. As will her Goodness." She offered me a hand, reluctantly, and helped me up. "I am going to tie you up nice and tight though," she said. "You can rest and heal. I'll send in Vae with herbs before sunset. Stave off any infection."

They left, and I slept fitfully, the smell of the slow-cooking stew tempting me awake every hour or so. But, after some time, it was not Vae who came in with herbs. It was Mahopi.

He set the wooden bowl of medicine on the table and turned to leave.

"Maho, I—"

"What?"

"I cannot reach that. Remember?"

"Oh."

He fetched the bowl and set it down on the bed next to me. "There."

"Oh. Um...thank you."

He made it three steps before turning back to me. "You can't reach that either, can you?"

"No...."

"Well, Vae is gone sheering, and Yahara is hunting. There is no one else around...."

"I can wait."

"No. Then infection will spread to your blood. It must be done before sunset. So says Gua." He leaned so he could peek out the door he left open. "Which...is now."

"You could release one of my hands."

"You might escape. Then Yahara will have my head."

"Watch me then."

"...Watch you?"

"It's just medicine, Maho. It's not like I am going to take off all my clothes and dance for you."

"You were barely wearing anything when they found you." He crossed his arms over his chest. "Just a man's shirt—"

"The sun is setting, as you said."

He sighed, then stepped forward and released one of my hands. His touch as his fingertips grazed my wrist was gentle. "Fine. I'm watching. From over here." He backed all the way up to the door and crossed his arms once more.

"Did...did Vae weave that shirt you're wearing?" I tried to make casual conversation as I scooped the herbs from the bowl and slid my hand up my dress. The motion revealed a good bit of my thigh and hip.

"She did," Maho said through clenched teeth.

"She's...getting good"—I hissed when I pressed too hard on the wound.

"She would be better if we didn't have to halt our entire lives to play soldiers." Maho crossed the room once more. "Just...give me that. You're terrible." He sat on the edge of the bed and took the bowl from me. "Lean back."

I obeyed, resting my head against the stuffed pillows behind me. I bit my lip as Maho eased up the hem of my dress, trying to pretend I did not remember what his hands felt like on dark nights when the moon was full and we'd had too much to drink.

"Relax," he said, dabbing the herbs on my wound. "I'm not going to jump on you. This is gross."

I grinned. "How did you know what I was thinking?"

He tried to hide his smile. "I'd like to believe I know you pretty well, Iz."

"Ha. I'm a mystery."

"And...I know that about you."

I snorted back my laugh.

But the moment passed, and Maho's face fell. "What if Yahara hadn't recognized you in the forest. You would have been dead, like that Cryl you were with."

"You think he's dead?" I did not entertain this thought. I'd seen Nkita Opas endure everything. Survive nine battles on the front lines. Live through losing his wing. A few Tru arrows wouldn't stop him. *Nothing will stop him from getting to me.*

"Of course he's dead. And if he's not...I will see to it that his end is my doing."

"Oh? You're a cold-blooded killer now, fish boy?"

He pretended his hands were pincers. "Ever seen me wrangle a lobster from the depths of the sea?" He brought those pincers closer and closer, threatening to attack me.

I put a warning finger up. "No. Mahopi, no. I am weak and injured. Be considerate."

"They call me Lobster Lord."

"No tickling! Don't you dare. We are very cross with each other, remember? *Remember?*"

He lowered his hand. "Oh. That's right."

"Mhmm. So now get out of here, before—"

"Before you fall in love with me. Again."

"Ah. He's gotten cocky too. So many new skills he's acquired, this Lobster Lord."

Maho surprised me by kissing my forehead. "Get some rest. And Vae and I will figure out how we're going to keep you safe."

He left me, and I'd just fallen asleep when something shoved me awake.

"Ow!"

"Get up," Yahara hissed. "Quietly. We can't let anyone find us."

"What...what are you—?"

"I'm taking you to the Queen. Tonight. Alone."

28

THE DAY THE SISTERS LEFT

"Limp faster."

I smacked away my sister's hand when she tried to grab me and pull me along. "This is as fast as I can hobble tonight. Be patient."

"The horses are just ahead. You do remember how to ride, yes?"

"I rode to deliver messages in the Capital. Also...I am still Tru, Yahara. Don't be mean."

"I am allowed to be as mean to you as I like."

"Fair."

In the moonlight, the land hummed in whispered tones. Through the trees, shafts of moonlight danced on the patches of snow, and the air smelled of frost and wet bark. The world of Miror had certainly been blessed by Gua, whether the Crylia chose to acknowledge it as we did or not.

"What a beautiful creature." I leaned against my new horse, patting its strong neck and glad, for once, to be able to express my love for the beasts without hiding my ways. "Will you carry me safely, friend?"

"His name is Bei." Yahara offered.

"I love him." His milky mane, white speckles, and tan coat glimmered as I stroked him.

"Well, you can't keep him. You are headed to your demise, remember?"

I sighed. "Can't you let me fantasize for a time? Hm?"

"You mean lie? Lie to yourself? And to this horse?"

"Yes. I mean lie." I studied the animal, trying to decide how I would climb up without ripping my wound open.

"Fine." Yahara said, offering me her palm so I could step up.

It still hurt like a thousand bee stings. But, I settled onto Bei's blanketed back and took the reins. "I know the way, Yayo. I can go myself."

"Nice try."

She led the way, her posture natural atop her beast. His name was Wen, and she'd loved him a long time. But the bow and quiver across her back, the blade beside them: those were new. *Tru were not meant to fight like this.*

"So tell me what happened, Iz. In Crylia."

"I thought you didn't care to know...."

"You're going to make me beg for the story, Storyteller?"

I grinned, the chilling breeze cool on my skin. "I served in the house of a white wing General at first. He was cruel and arrogant. And the slavemaster's name was Old Zloy. She was wicked as well, for the most part. But I did make a friend. Nolyen. A gray wing."

"You left her behind?"

"It was for the best. And also an accident. But when the old General was killed, a new one took his place. A Teth to the Cza and a First General."

"Opas. The Terrible."

"Yes. And he found me out in an instant. In a moment. One glance, and he knew."

"That doesn't sound possible, Iz."

"I have no other explanation. If there is one, it eludes me. But this Nkita, he offered to keep my secret if I agreed to spy for him as well."

"What need did he have for a spy among his own ranks?"

"I thought at first that it would serve him politically. The Teth are a nasty lot when it comes to trading secrets and amassing power."

"But that is not what you think now?"

"No. I think he wanted to have an ear to the ground because his bloodline is pure. Close to the Cza's. It was a secret that put him in danger. He needed to know who was on to him at all times. But then...."

"Do not say you fell in love. Don't."

"It happened so fast, Yayo."

"Blech."

"And there was torture and pain and fear...but also laughter and courage and devotion. I did not know a being could be so loyal to another. Not until Nkita."

"*You* are the judge of loyalty now?"

I sighed. "What have you been up to since I was sent away?"

Yahara shrugged. "Fighting off Cryl trying to cross the border. Waiting. Waiting some more."

"Waiting...?"

"For you to come home."

"And now...."

"Now, no more waiting."

We rode in silence the rest of the way. And when the Royal Home appeared before us, rising up above the hillside in green and brown, like the mountain itself had built the structure, I wished we'd talked about happy things. About the brothers we'd lost and the way we missed our parents. About the family we'd forged out of ill-trained soldiers and effort. About Gua. About mercy and kindness.

But my mate was coming. And he would remove anyone who stood between us. He wouldn't understand. They wouldn't understand. So I would have to understand for both sides.

I pulled up on Bei, took a deep breath, and said the words so my sister would not have to. "Emyri Izela of the Tru. I am here to speak with the Queen regarding my imminent execution."

29

THE DAY THE QUEEN KNELT

The Home of the Queen had changed since I'd last walked its halls.

Where before there were tapestries of gold and white, now slabs of metal meant to act as shields lined the walls. The soft grass permitted to grow along the floors of the Home should still have been growing, even in the cold months, but it had been replaced by sharp gravel. *So the guards can hear if someone is coming in the dead of night.*

The attendants and advisers all whispered when they saw me. They knew me, of course. The Tru-Ori who had been treasured by the late King. For a time.

When I was taken to the Queen's Hall, I expected to be permitted my dignity, as was the custom. But I was shoved to my knees, my hip groaning in pain.

Yahara stepped back and off to the side. I wished she would leave, but my sister and I had received double portions of obstinance from Gua, it seemed.

We waited. Waited for the Queen to arrive. But before she did, the fires were lit and the slow rumble of drums filled my ears.

Then...she came.

She wore white, her gown flowing down in layers from her thin shoulders. I often wondered how she appeared to be dressed and ready for visits at any time. *Does she sleep in these gowns?* In all my years, I had never seen her more casual. Not even while she bathed in the rivers.

"What have we here?" she asked, her voice smooth and gentle, her tear-shaped face narrow and small. Her dark blue hair was almost purple, her eyes a surprising gold to denote her wisdom—both Tru-hana and Tru-ori in one.

"It is the traitor, Emyri Ize"—a man spoke up.

"I know who she is, adviser, thank you. I mean to ask why she is present."

"I have no knowledge of that, Good Queen."

"Then why are you so eager to speak up if you are not the one with information I can make use of?" She spoke with such grace, but her words cut deep, and the adviser grimaced.

If I were not about to be killed, I would have smirked. The Queen had always been my favorite.

"I found her in the woods," Yahara said. "During patrol."

The Queen held up a hand to silence my sister. "I will speak with Izela alone."

Yahara took a deep, audibly fragile breath. "May I petition on her behalf?"

Oh Yahara.... My eyes pricked with tears. She had done the same when I was convicted the first time around. And it wouldn't do her any good now either.

"I will speak with Izela. Alone." The Queen waited, her eyes downcast as the room cleared. Then, she tapped her personal guard on the forearm. "You too, Pino."

The guard, displaying his guardsman scars proudly on his bare chest, stood as still as ever, his nostrils flaring, his grip tightening on his spear. "I will not leave my Queen's side."

She sighed. "Must you be so insistent?"

"You will have to drive a blade through my skull to be rid of me."

"Very well. You may stay." She nodded and stepped forward. There was no pedestal between her and the people, as there was with the Cza of Crylia. She was not above. She was the same.

"We may speak freely," she said. And then, she knelt before me so we were eye to eye. And wrapped her arms around my neck. "I missed you."

I could not help it. Sobs shook me as I held onto her. "I missed you so much, Miasi."

She held me at arms length, her hands on my cheeks. "Were you hurt? Was it dreadful? How did you survive it?"

I placed my hands over hers. "One day at a time. And with quite a bit of help." I shook my head. "I worried every day for you. For all of you."

"I know, Izzy."

"I...I did not think...."

"You did not think I would still love you?" She put a hand to my chest. "Izela, you *saved my life*."

"That is not how—"

"That is what happened. It's the truth."

"I killed the *King*, Miasi. There is no redemption for me in this story. No way out."

"Oh come on, Storyteller. We have employed great creativity to keep you from being killed for treason. We can come up with something once more."

"Miasi, I cannot remain here in the Royal Home. There is something I must tell you. Someone—"

A commotion outside the Queen's Hall, and my entire body stiffened. My arms and legs went weak after that, my heart rattling, my breath quickening. I could feel him. Coming closer but somehow already inside me. Deep in my bones. In my soul.

I mourned and rejoiced. I desired and feared.

"The General," I whispered to no one. To anyone. To Gua. "He's here." *And he will kill everyone I love to get to me if I don't do something. Now.*

30

THE DAY THE CRYL ATTACKED

"An intruder?" Miasi did not have time to stand on her feet before Pino was to her.

The giant of a man hoisted her to her feet and stood between her and the commotion, spear drawn.

I could not find the words to display my absolute dread. *Yahara. What if they cross swords? Nkita will rend her in half.* I shuddered when I imagined his talons sinking into her abdomen, my name on her lips as she died. *Move your legs, Em. Go. Do something.* But all that came from me was one sentiment, one realization. "This is my fault."

"Crylia!" someone shouted from outside the Hall. *Of course it's a Crylia.* And he would have no mercy. *Maybe I can tell him to stop. To stand down. But then...he will be slaughtered. He can't even take flight and escape, and that's also....* "This is all my fault." *Gua. Help.*

Miasi looked at me with wide eyes. "You...you did this?" She wrestled with Pino, determined to remain in the room with me a little longer.

I shook my head, forcing words past the lump in my throat. "No...Miasi...that's not what I mean...."

"You *led them here*, Izela?"

I dug my fingers into my hair, praying to Gua that time would slow.

"I trusted you. I have always trusted you!"

"We must flee, my Queen," Pino said, his voice so deep it frightened me.

Miasi shoved Pino until he stopped trying to drag her. "No, Pino. Go! Go to the Tonguekeeper. Protect her at all costs."

The...the Tonguekeeper?

"I will not leave your side, Queen Miasi..." the guard replied.

I stood to my feet, raising my voice so it could be heard above our panic. "Listen to me. No harm will come to anyone. I will *fix this*. The one who has come...he is looking for me. He is my—"

But the Crylia who broke down the door of the Queen's Hall wore white wings. His sword gleamed in the firelight as he spread his stance. Blood dropped from his blade, pooling at his feet.

"Kneel before the Hresh. And point us to the Tongue-keeper if you wish for your Queen to take another breath."

I stumbled backward, bumping into Pino.

"You know this Cryl, Izela?" Miasi whispered.

"No." I licked my dry lips and clenched my fists. "And yes. I have been hiding the Tonguekeeper. Forgive me for keeping this secret from you, Queen Miasi. Forgive me."

Before the Queen could object to my deception, I shared a glance with Pino. Then, with everything I had in me, I raced toward the white wing Hresh, allowing time for Pino and Miasi to escape if it were not for the second and third Hresh who appeared, spreading their wings and snagging Pino with their talons. In full Crylia form, their white fur covered their forearms and necks, and their scarlet eyes glowed like fire rubies.

The Hresh nearest me took hold of my throat, sending me crashing to the floor, my shoulder smashing the ground and pain flooding my body.

"Don't"—I tried to scream, reaching for Miasi in an effort to protect her.

Pino lunged his spear into the shoulder of the second Hresh, causing him to howl in pain. But he was no match for two Cryl at once, and the third Hresh ripped at Pino's skull with his talons until there was nothing left.

Miasi's scream filled the Queen's Hall as she rushed to her guard's side.

And just as the white wing reached for the Tru Queen, Kieli Yahara slid into the room, snatched the Queen with her, and raced out the other side of the Hall.

"Find them!" screeched the Hresh who held me fast. "I will squeeze the location of the Tonguekeeper from this one. Bring me the Queen of the Tru. Alive."

The remaining Hresh nodded and flew through the doors, seeking out Yahara and Miasi.

I was alone with the first white wing.

He wasted no time, slamming his fist into my belly. Once, twice. Three times, until I could not breathe. He gripped my face with his palm and brought my head down onto the ground until I felt as though my skull would crack.

"Tell me," he said, moving so he choked me, his knee pressing on my chest. "Where is the Tonguekeeper?"

As the Queen's guards filtered into the room, the Hresh demolished them, one after the other. Every time I tried to flee, he was on me, dragging me back. Finally, he took off with me. His wings pushed him off the ground. I was hoisted, screaming and clawing, into the air until he thrust my back into the ceiling. The branches of the old Tru trees growing there crushed my ribs, my spine.

The Hresh used one of my people's swords, weaving it through the branches and over my midsection so I was pinned in place. If I did not hold to the branches with my shaking hands, my body would have flopped in half, the sides of the sword slicing into me.

I watched. I watched as one by one, the Tru guardsmen and guardswomen were killed. Blood pooled around the white wing's shoes and he worked as if he did not care, slicing and hacking with finesse.

Think, Em. Think. How can you get down? How can you get out? But my head throbbed, and when I coughed, I tasted copper.

At last, the Palace was still. If there were more guards, they'd either fled or hidden themselves. At least the killing had stopped. The white wing turned his head to me, about to take flight, no doubt prepared to continue his 'questioning'.

It was then that a well-aimed arrow took the back of the Cryl.

I knew that arrow. *Yahara.*

"Run!" I shrieked, my body convulsing as I held myself in place. "Please! Run!" *Don't be brave. Not today. Get out. Protect the Queen and go—*

In horror—in absolute *agony*—I watched as the Hresh plunged his sword into my sister. And all would have been lost if not for the silent shadow that filled the room.

When he entered, time moved aside. Energy itself bowed before him. He did not have to flourish his blade or let out a warrior's cry. He stepped with the confidence of deity into the Queen's Hall, his black cloak following behind him.

Nkita Opas stood ready, the soles of his boots planted in the blood of my people, and raised his sword.

31

THE DAY THE BLOOD RAN RED

The clashing of swords, the sparking of metal and fury. The monsters raged in heated battle.

Backing away, the white wing scoffed. "Grand Teth Nkita. You find yourself in such common places these days."

Nkita circled the Hresh, his lavender irises nothing but slivers in his eyes. He said nothing. Only stared at his opponent.

"A wonder you made it this far, seeing that the Cza saw it fit to pluck one of your little wings."

He meant to rile Nkita up. And perhaps it would have worked on a white wing. But it had no effect on the General. The power coming from his body made mine throb. He knew what he wanted. And it was death.

It took ten more seconds and two more moves before Nkita's blade came down on the head of the Hresh with such precision that his face became two, split in half down the middle.

He looked up to me at once. "Hold," was all he said. "I'm coming."

Quickly, he took the bow from my fallen sister, turning her so he could retrieve an arrow as well. "Inhale on three," he instructed, aiming the arrow up at me. "One, two...three." Then, he let the arrow fly. It snapped one of the branches holding the sword, and down I came.

In a moment, Nkita had me in his arms. But there was no time for romance. "How many Hresh?"

I gasped, trying to find my breath and my words as he set me down.

He took to one knee as I crumpled, holding my face in his hands and studying my eyes. He slid his hand to the back of my head and pulled away to find blood on his hands. "Damn, Em." He stood. "Two? Three of them?"

I nodded my head, my brain on fire as I did so.

"Stay. And *don't die*."

Then he was off, his sword in hand.

I had every intention of staying. And not dying. Until I heard a whimper come from my sister's body. *Yahara? Alive?* Anguish sought to hold me back, but I crawled, my chest and belly dragging across the floor. Past the bodies of the fallen until I found my family.

I placed my hands on her bleeding wound and laid my head next to hers. *Not yet, Gua.* I begged the goddess of the water. *Not yet. Let her stay longer in this world. Let her stay with me.* My tears bathing us both, I held on as long as I could. And when the darkness came for me, I wished it would be kind, as Gua was kind. Gracious as she was gracious. And that she would leave my sister where she met her. In my arms. Alive.

I awoke to someone shaking my shoulders and pleading with me.

"Wake up, Izela! Please! Please!" Miasi's usually smooth voice broke as she pleaded. "Izzy!"

I coughed, my eyes fluttering open. And then groaned. "Mia, no. No shaking."

"Oh, thank Gua!" She sobbed, her forehead to mine, her deep blue hair fluttering around me.

I tried to sit up, propping myself on my elbows. "Yahara!"

"She is alright. Very grumpy, though." Miasi frowned. "She smacked a guard for not helping her up fast enough."

"Up? Sh-she should be resting. Help me up. I will get her to sit down."

"You are both too stubborn to bear."

Miasi helped me sit up, and I took stock of the carnage. So many dead. So many dying.

"Did you see the black wing, Miasi? Did you see where he went?"

"He's here."

Nkita's voice made the room gasp. Miasi stood slowly, making sure not to cower before the black wing as he approached.

She took a deep breath. "You...saved my life, Crylia."

170

He growled, nodding his head toward me. "Blame her."

Miasi looked over at me, her brow furrowed. "Izela?"

"She makes me do these things."

"Stop whining and help me up," I told him.

He scoffed. "You need rest."

"I am bored of rest. Yahara is permitted to walk around. Why not me?"

"Don't know who that is. Don't care. She's not mine. You are."

Miasi put her head in her hands and sighed. "I am beyond exhausted. I must be...I must be delusional. Or...."

"Rest if you want," Nkita said to the Queen. "But again. I don't care." Nkita hoisted me up into his arms without straining. "I'll find you a bed, Em."

"There are beds right here," I told him. "Put me back down."

"Em. We—"

"Em?" Miasi squeezed her eyes shut in disbelief. "You have affectionately shortened her name? What is going on?"

Yahara shouted out from across the hall, leaning on the wall and clearly worn out. "She didn't tell you, Queen Miasi? She's been sitting on this one's member!"

"What?" Miasi said, her mouth open, her eyes wide as she turned to me. "Is this true?"

"He's my mate, Good Queen—"

"Your mate? Emyri Izela. That was not part of your assignment."

171

"I...love him."

Nkita gave an arrogant chuckle. I felt it vibrate against my side as he held me in his arms.

"Hush, you."

Miasi studied us with careful eyes. "I find myself in a precarious situation. Due to the war between our people and the Crylia, I am sworn to defend the Tru against your kind, monster. But...."

"You own me your life, Queen?" Nkita said.

"I do."

"Keep your life debt. I want no part of it. What I do wish to know is what the Hresh were after. Perhaps we may discuss this while Em rests—"

While I rest? "No. Absolutely not. You think I will be put to sleep like a small child while the adults discuss the important things?" I glared up at Nkita. "Over my dead body."

"That's what *I* said!" Yahara called out, still across the room, still too exhausted to do much and too hard headed to admit it.

Miasi gave a quiet smile. "I propose this solution. We will all rest, bathe, tend to our wounds, perhaps weep in private, and then reconvene to discuss what has happened. Any objections to this plan?"

Yahara pointed at Nkita. "The Cryl gets to rest in the Palace?" she said with a scowl.

"Yahara, I do believe that if he meant to harm us, he wouldn't require stealth at this point. What would be the reason for doubting his intentions now?"

"He's *Crylia*."

"He is. And until I decide what will be done with him, he will bathe and rest just as we will. He will drink our herbs alongside us and mend. And do not take my tone as submissive, Yahara. I assure you it is not."

Yahara swallowed. "My apologies, Good Queen."

"It is alright. You are understandably protective. Now. Go. All of you. And...forgive my attendants for not being able to prepare rooms at the moment. There is much to be done." She looked around at the bodies. "Much loss to be accounted for."

"Leave the white wings for me, Queen of the Tru," Nkita said. "I will investigate them. See what I can find."

She nodded. "Consider it done."

Nkita left with me, and as soon as we were out of earshot, he whispered into my hair. "Go to sleep, trouble-maker. I'll keep watch."

32

THE DAY THE HEART BEAT

The sun never knows it's supposed to be sad. It shines like nothing terrible has ever happened. Gua says when it leaves us, when it sleeps, it forgets the events of the day before. Forgetful sun, always shining.

But the water...she remembers. She holds.

I eased myself up with great effort to find Nkita wide awake. He sat on the floor, his back against the wall and his body angled toward the door. He flipped through a book in that early morning light.

"Are you...are you *reading*?"

"No," he grumbled. "Go back to sleep."

"What about you? I have no doubt you're exhausted. Come and lie down."

"Your consideration is pointless."

I sighed. "May I tend to your wounds."

He slapped the book closed and turned those stunning lilac eyes to me. "Must you make me repeat myself so often? Is this what life with you will truly be like? As I said not even a moment ago...your consideration is pointless."

I scowled. "You will not only *allow* me to be considerate of you, Nkita Black Wing, but you will be *grateful* for it. And in time, mark my words, you will *crave* it."

I winced my way out of bed and crossed the small room, sitting cross-legged in front of my mate.

"I am to be guarding the door," he argued as I began undressing him.

"Then guard it." I pulled the belt from his trousers and tossed it over my shoulder. Then, I took the hem of his shirt in my hands. "Hands up."

He snarled. "No."

I narrowed my eyes at him, which only made my head ache worse. "Don't make me hurt you, First General."

"Ha. With those slender little hands?"

"I will have you know, I was trained in the foundry of the great Grand Teth Nkita Opas. These hands are quite skilled."

The corner of his mouth twitched. "Your master must have done a shite job. You got your arse handed to you last night."

I shrugged. "I didn't want to show off. Would have frightened the Hresh."

"Mm. They would have trembled before you?"

"Yes. And I prefer to slay my enemy while their dignity is still intact."

175

"Yet you will not allow me to keep mine?"

"Hands up, or else. I mean it."

He sighed and obliged, letting me slide his worn shirt off him. Since last I'd seen my mate, his bruises had multiplied, spreading across both of his shoulders. His ribs were purple and black, scars crisscrossing beneath fresh wounds.

"Nkita...."

"What?"

"Stay here—"

When I tried to get up, he pulled me back down. "Where do you think you're going?"

"To...to get help. Our herbs will—"

"I'm not letting you out of my sight, Emyri."

"At least let me fetch fresh bandages—"

"You're really that worried about me?"

I nodded, only then realizing I was gripping his legs tight as I sat before him.

"Then I will tell you what I really need."

"Name it."

He reached out and put his hand on my back, pulling me forward until my head rested on his chest.

I unfolded my legs and turned them to one side, wrapping my arms around his torso and letting my cheek melt against his skin.

"I...won't hurt you?"

"No. Just...." He sighed, his tense muscles relaxing one at a time. "I need you. I haven't been able to convince you of that. Not yet. But it's the truest thing about me, Em."

He tucked my hair behind my ear before he exhaled and leaned his head back against the wall. If he had his way, he would never have slept. He would have kept alert and awake, minding the door and pretending a book could keep his eyes from closing. But with me near him, sleep came whether he liked it or not.

I sat as still as I could, listening to the quick rhythm of his heart beating against my temple, the slow rise and fall of his breathing.

Gua...thank you for bringing him back to me, I prayed. *Thank you.*

When I thought he was deep enough into his sleep, I inched away. He groaned when I left him, but his eyes stayed closed, his fingers twitching as if his soul knew I was going.

"I'll be right back," I whispered to him. "I promise."

I sneaked out the door and hobbled along until I found the Queen's Chambers.

33

THE DAY THE TRU REMEMBERED

"Come in," Miasi said before I could knock.

I entered, standing just inside the door and closing it behind me. I took a deep breath before I spoke. "Are you alright, Mia?"

"I am well. A few bumps and bruises, but nothing serious."

I nodded. "I...am so sorry about Pino."

"Yes. He was devoted. And I will miss him greatly."

"Shall...we pray?"

"Another time."

I figured she would not want to grieve, but it was right for me to ask. "I cannot stay long, or Nkita will come looking for me."

"I understand."

I swallowed, leaning back against the door. When no one else was around, I could speak to her like the friends we were. "Do you really have the Tonguekeeper here, Mia?"

She frowned. "I did. But it appears...she is gone."

"You were using her?"

Miasi balked, surprised at my insinuation. "Of course not. I was tasked with protecting her. And it seems I have failed. When I went to find her after the Crylia attacked, to see that she was safe...."

"And she was missing."

"Yes. But if she was taken by the Crylia, why would they come looking for her?"

"They wouldn't." I chewed the inside of my cheek as I thought. "Would anyone else have taken her?"

"I keep her existence secret, Iz. But...rumors claim that the Czas of the Crylia have suspected for hundreds of years that we harbor her. Perhaps that is why they target our people more keenly. Why they wage war with us so intently, more so than with other human tribes."

"We are a naturally peaceful people. We have always wondered why they hate us, why they want to destroy us so fully. Why not the warrior tribes on their other border? Or the Magdi to our south, with their great wealth and resources? But you are saying all of this...all of this carnage is because we are protecting one person?"

"Perhaps. There are many theories. That is one of them."

"If she is so important—"

"There is no one more important in all of Miror than that one being."

My breath caught. "Then...we must find her."

"Before the Cza."

"Yes. Before the Great Cza." Miasi paused, her mind drifting. "Did...you ever glimpse him, Iz? The Great Cza?"

"Mm. He was at our wedding."

"Gua bless you. And is he truly so cruel as they say? More wicked than even his Generals?"

"Yes, Miasi. But you will never have to face him. Not as long as I live."

She smiled, but her eyes were sad. "My tribe of warriors will protect me?"

"We will do what we can. For Tru. For you."

"We are changing. Before my very eyes. Our gentle ways traded for the path of the sword and arrow." She straightened her shoulders. "Nonetheless. We have a task to see to the end. Do you think your...black wing... would assist?"

"I will tell you this in confidence...."

"Of course. I will hold whatever it is between us."

"He is no ordinary black wing, Miasi. Nkita Opas is the Pureblood Heir to the throne of Crylia. He has the right to challenge the Cza. So far, he has fled from this truth. But I know the rebel Crylia are looking for him, seeking him out to fight on their behalf. To free Crylia from the Cza's oppression."

"You tell me this because I should consider the black wing...occupied?"

"I tell you this because, if he is willing, we might seek his aid in more ways than one."

"You think he can help us find the Tonguekeeper...and that we should rally behind him to defeat the Cza?" Miasi thought about this, folding in her lips, her long slender neck turning her head toward her window. "I am wary of using what little strength our militia has left...all to put another Crylia on the throne."

"You think the Tru can win the war against Crylia, Miasi?"

She gave a bitter chuckle. "Of course not."

"Then...what future could be better than the one outlined for us? Where at least, for a time, the new Cza may honor his word and be sympathetic toward the Tru that fought to get him on the throne?"

"I will consider that option, Izela. For now, let us see if we can gather the forces—and the courage—to locate our Tonguekeeper in time. For if we cannot find her, there will be no Tru left to protect. All of Miror will be lost."

"I will go to Nkita. However...do you have any bandages, Miasi? Water? Or—"

"Of course. Forgive me, I will find some for you. And why don't you sit there in the bath for a time while I look. I just drew the water myself. It's warm."

"Queen Mia—"

"Sit. Bathe. Rest. I will lay out something for you to wear that's not covered in blood and filth." She snapped her fingers. "And herbs. To speed the mending of the wounds of you both."

The Queen began searching for items of healing, and I marveled at her ways. At our ways. In Tru, even the Queen served alongside her people. The Cza in his high throne would never look for bandages for his enemy.

I gave my thanks to her and hurried back to my room. Well...I could not hurry, but I did return. And I slipped back into Nkita's arms and closed my eyes.

"You think you're clever, don't you?"

I jumped, but he held me fast, his arm pressing me toward him. "When do I get to undress you? Check on all your wounds?"

"Nkita—"

"Fair is fair."

"We must first discuss a very important matter—"

"No. I discuss nothing until you're undressed."

He stood, pulling me up with him. Then, he walked me backwards toward the bed. "You will cooperate."

"I will do as you ask if you also do what I ask. How is that for cooperation?"

"Deal."

Then, Nkita pulled my woolen dress over my head without hesitation. He sucked in air when he saw me. "Emyri Izela. Why do you never listen to me, hm?"

"Oh? Like when you led me into Tru territory and then had your way with me on a boulder until my own unit shot us through with arrows? Listen to you like that, General?"

"If I squint just right and ignore the bruises...." He laid me back on the bed. "You're still beautiful."

"Trying to distract me with pretty words, now."

"I will have no trouble distracting you. Begin your rambling about important matters. And I will remind you of why you're never going to run away from me again."

"Well...I visited with the Queen and"—I gasped as he slipped his hand along the inside of my thigh, tracing his fingers carefully downward.

"Go on."

"And...she was the...th-the keeper—"

He followed the trail his finger had made with a mixture of kisses and bites.

"Do all you Cryl have such sharp teeth?" I hissed, arching my back as if that would somehow change anything.

"You will never know." He bit me harder, and I shivered.

"Be nice!"

"Mm...no. I don't think I will."

He took his time, his lips working while mine struggled to form words.

"I...she...the keeper of the...th-the Tongue"—I gasped, taking a fistful of his hair in my hand. "Not *your* tongue!"

But he only stroked his tongue more confidently until I shook beneath his grasp. He ignored the knock at the door. And when whoever it was entered our room, he ignored that too. All I heard was a cry and the person stumbling back out again, closing the door firmly behind them.

Do not cry, Em. Do not. No crying, no moaning. Hold yourself together. Hold—

I arched my back so fully that I might have rolled right off the bed if he did not keep his grip on me. Then, he eased away and kissed my mouth fully.

"There," he said, looking into my eyes. "*My* mate."

"Mmm...."

Blood rushed to every inch of my body, and everything around me vanished when he looked into my eyes like that. As if he saw me. Every insecurity and flaw. Every grace and strength. As if I satisfied him just by existing.

"You will remember?" He took my throat in his hands, feeling for my pulse. "Say it, Em."

I nodded.

"Say it out loud. I need to hear it." He lifted his chin, waiting.

I took a shuddering breath as I placed my hand around his throat. "I will remember."

34

The Day The Three Assembled

"What?" Nkita asked, nearly ripping the door off its hinges. I'd barely gotten my dress over my head.

My sister's voice responded. "Don't be ugly, Crylia. I knocked."

"And...? *What?*"

"The Queen. She is requesting an audience with all of us. Now."

"You must understand, small human, that I do not answer to you. You understand this, yes?"

"Listen, you *pointy-fingered, snake-eyed feather boy.* I don't give a damn about you. But that girl in there? She's *my* little sister. Not yours. Mine."

I could feel Nkita smile without being able to see it.

Oh, that's not good. That's a danger smile. I limped between them, standing in the doorway. "Let's all go see what the Queen needs."

Yahara's cheeks were flaming, her eyes bloodshot with fury. "You have words now, hm? Couldn't have given me a 'hold on' or a 'come back later', Izela? Let me walk in on...on all that?" she huffed. "This is the worst day of my life."

"Focus on the task at hand." I pushed her forward.

"You need a bath."

"Onward, Yahara."

"Did he even wash his face when he was through?"

To my surprise and horror, Nkita ran his tongue over his lips. "No need."

"Gua, send rain. Let's not keep Miasi waiting and all agree to walk in *silence* until we arrive."

We made it to the Queen's Hall without breaking into a duel. The bodies had all been cleared except for the two dead Hresh. The third body was yet to be recovered.

The Queen was waiting for us, as regal as ever in a fresh white gown. She inclined her head to Nkita. "I have heard of you, great General."

"I was once a General, yes. But I am no longer in service to the Cza."

"Well, you may examine the bodies of the Cryl, as you wished."

Nkita got to work, and Miasi continued.

"We must prepare a strategy. To recover the Tonguekeeper—"

"Is that what you were going on about earlier?" Nkita asked, looking up at me from where he crouched over the dead Hresh.

"Shh! The Queen is speaking." I blushed, nodding at Miasi. "Please go on."

Miasi went on. "Yes. We need to find her. And...I am hoping the three of you can assist me on this quest."

"Of course. I am honored," Yahara said. "I will need to know what a Tonguekeeper...*is*...but—"

"She is only choosing you because all her guards are either dead or cowards." Nkita stood up with a scowl. "It's no honor."

Yahara scowled, crossing his arms. "I could not hate him more, Izela."

But it was Miasi who stepped forward. "Do not place words in my mouth, nor profess to know the sentiments of my heart, black wing." She held Nkita's gaze without flinching, her head high.

Nkita, finally, inclined his. "Very well."

"I have another request, General."

"Speak it."

"I will ask it once the Tonguekeeper is safely recovered."

"Suit yourself."

I spoke up. "...Good Queen."

Everyone angled toward me.

I cleared my throat. "She is to be addressed as 'Good Queen'.

Nkita stared at me, and I glared back at him.

"Is...the meeting over," he asked, "*Good Queen*?"

"It is not," the Queen said. "General, I ask that you please work together with Yahara and her unit to recover the Tonguekeeper."

"What? Queen Miasi, you cannot be serious," Yahara said, dropping both her arms and her jaw. "We cannot...we cannot traipse around Tru with a *monster*!"

"You can and you will."

"I will do as you ask," Nkita answered, his gaze still as stone. "For Em."

I watched and waited while Yahara loudly stated everything wrong with Miasi's plan. But I understood it. She was testing Nkita. To see if he could indeed work with the Tru people. And if he could, she would put her weight behind him so he could pursue the Cza's crown.

But that was not what weighed on my shoulders, what kept my mouth closed and my eyes downcast.

Finally, Miasi called for silence. Then, she looked to me. "Emyri Izela. You have been very quiet. What is the reason for your restraint?"

"It is a selfish reason, Good Queen. I will keep it to myself."

"Em is never selfish," Nkita said, his voice cool. "But she is rarely honest."

Miasi studied Nkita, then nodded at me. "Go on. Your concern may be pertinent to us all."

"I...I do not think it would be wise for me to travel through Tru, Queen Miasi. I may not be well received."

"It's true," Yahara said. "They will see her as a traitor. Since that is what she is."

Nkita looked across to me but he said nothing.

Yahara scoffed. "Oh? She didn't tell you she's a traitor to all of Tru, black wing? Yes, *high* treason."

"Enough," Miasi said. "Izela, you are needed."

"And what of my trial?" I asked.

"Trials can wait. One thing at a time, Izela. Find the Tonguekeeper. Save Miror."

35

The Day The Cryl Rode

"The Queen has lost her mind. She is rattled from all this violence and is making questionable decisions." Yahara marched off in search of our horses.

"*She* has lost her mind?" Nkita grumbled. "You have left your weaponry behind, Commander."

Yahara scoffed. "You mean my bow? It was sullied by the hands of a Crylia. I'll need a new one."

We found our horses grazing a ways out from the Home of the Queen, and Nkita paused. "Shall I walk?"

It was not the first time I wondered if he missed his wing, but it was the first time I was certain he longed for it. "Ride with me," I told him. "You can keep me company."

I held up my palm so that Bei came to rub his nose against it. The steed leaned his tawny body against me for an embrace.

"You two have been friends a long time?" Nkita asked.

"No, we just met," I explained.

"Yet, he leans against you as if you raised him."

I grinned at the Crylia. "I'm Tru, General. We love horses."

"I think it is horses that love you."

I was about to swing my aching body onto Bei's back when Nkita hoisted me up, his strong hands tight around my waist. I nudged my way forward so he could climb up behind me. Bei complained about the added weight until I pet his neck.

"Your sister is long gone," Nkita pointed out. "She is the impatient sort."

"Impatient and angry. She hates when I keep secrets from her. And you were a big one."

"She banishes you to the life of a spy and then complains when she cannot hear from you?"

"My punishment is not Yahara's fault, Nkita. It's mine." I urged Bei on, leaning back against my mate's chest.

The sun had broken over the hills, green grass poking out from beneath patches of white snow. The blue sky sang out for Gua, white clouds dancing over the trees.

"It is more temperate here," Nkita remarked. "And we are not that far from Crylia. How odd."

"Gua is not odd," I explained. "She helps the helpless, is all."

Nkita scoffed. "You think a water goddess brings you warm weather?"

"She blesses us whether you believe she does or not."

"Mm." He inched forward so I could feel every part of him pressing against my rear.

"Must you always desire me?"

"I must." He paused, taking in the view as we moved toward the unit along the border. "You told the Queen about me."

"I...yes. I did."

"I am surprised you are being honest with me, Em."

"You are not cross I told her about your bloodline?"

"I have nothing to fear from Queen Miasi of the Tru! She may know whatever she likes."

I bristled. "Because we are so weak? We could never harm you?"

"Because I can feel her heart beating in my chest as surely as I feel yours. And your sister's. And every Tru who lay dying on the ground in the Palace. They are gentle. And...good." Then he reached for the reins, taking them from my hands. "But we will need to hide me, won't we? When we wander through Tru?"

"Nkita, I don't think such a thing is possible. You are taller than any Tru—and we are not short people—and with broad shoulders and hair so black, it makes me nervous. You have the sharp nose of a Crylia, not to mention a wing that is quite obvious, even when you keep it tucked. You even walk like a Cryl. There can be no hiding you, General."

"I did not mean it that way."

"What did you mean then?"

"I will have to hide...my nature. My instincts. Or I will frighten all who see me, and we will accomplish nothing."

"And this task is truly important to you? Finding the Tonguekeeper?"

"Truly? No. It is not my destiny. But perhaps it is yours. So I will lend my aid. And my sword. And my body."

"Your body, eh?"

He leaned forward, kissing my neck. "Comes at a bargain." He traced his lips upward until he reached my jaw.

"I should teach you how to behave. So you are ready." I needed to distract him or I would come off this horse and let him take me to the ground.

"I will find my own way."

"Alright then. Let's say my friend Cevae asks for you to come in and sit down, share a meal with her. What do you say?"

"I can hunt my own food."

"Nkita, no! That would be terribly insulting. Try again."

He groaned. "Fine. I would accept her invitation."

"Wrong again."

"So I cannot say no and I cannot say yes?"

"Precisely."

"No wonder the Tru are losing the war."

I elbowed him. "Nkita!"

"Alright, alright. What do I say?"

"You say that you must make amends with Yahara first. She is our Commander, and we cannot sit down together if there is strife between you."

"So each of your nests has a Commander?"

"No, no. Each of our families has an elder. A head. Not to be in charge and give orders, usually, but to ensure we are keeping the peace of the family. They serve as a mediator, a counselor, a keeper of Gua's sayings. For my family, it was my grandmother. But now...things are different. And since we are not with our families, since we are a unit, we must hold to our traditions as best we can."

"So...this Yahara is the wise one of your unit?"

I sighed. "Yes."

"You truly were not designed for militant lives."

"We are not."

"Oh, and I will not be making amends with her so...."

"I thought you wanted to blend in!"

"...Fine."

When we arrived at the base camp, nestled in the last valley before the Crylia border, Cevae waved at a distance, running up to us.

"This must be your friend."

I grinned. "Yes. You will like her."

Cevae stopped running, her smile slipping off her tan face, her hand lowering.

"If you say so," Nkita grunted.

We dismounted, Nkita lifting me down to the ground, and I crossed the remaining distance to Cevae, wrapping her in my arms.

She held on tight. "You're alive."

"For now. Very much so."

"Yahara told us what happened. Well...she mostly yelled and threw things around her home, but I caught some of it." Then Cevae leaned in, whispering. "That's...that's a black wing, isn't it, Iz?"

"This is Nkita. My...my mate."

"That's the same one from the forest—ohhh. Oh dear." She swallowed, her eyes wide. Then, she turned on her heel. "Better go! Have some weaving to do before patrol—"

"Not so fast," I said, hooking my arm in hers and turning her back around. "Come meet him. I will need your help convincing the others he's nice."

I dragged her over, and she stood shaking, licking her lips and wringing her hands.

It didn't help that the General refused to crack even the slightest smile.

"Cevae, this is Nkita. Nkita, my friend Cevae.

Cevae gave an awkward nod. "The...the water suits you, Nkita."

Nkita narrowed his eyes. "Does it?"

I shot him a look. "You must reply, The rivers are yours, Cevae."

"I highly doubt she owns any of these rivers. But alright."

I waited. We all waited. "Nkita. Say it."

He sighed. "The rivers are yours, Cevae."

Cevae shook her head. "Blessed by a Cryl. Never in all my days. Gua must be chuckling."

I bit my lip, glaring at Nkita, lest he say some nonsense like, "To chuckle, Gua would have to exist."

"So...you are accompanying us on a new quest? We've had very little questing as a unit, to be honest. We are not the strongest fighters. We scout alright. That's why we are here, near the border." Cevae smiled at me. "Izzy is always riding around, carrying information for other units. And reporting to Queen Miasi." Her smile vanished. "Well...she was. But—"

"Let us gather what we need and get going," I told my Tru-ori friend. "We have a lot of work to do."

"Do we have a description of this...Tonguekeeper?" Cevae asked, headed with us toward the little gathering of homes. "That might help."

"The Queen gave us few details. She said the Tonguekeeper preferred not to be seen or heard. She lived peacefully in a cave near the Palace, taking no visitors. So...we will have to look for someone powerful and secretive."

"How are we going to find someone secretive?"

"You would be surprised, Vae. When the world is loud, quiet people stand out quite clearly. Sometimes, secrets scream."

"Says the one who harbors more secrets than she has bones," Nkita said.

"I would know," I snapped at him. "I am an expert at hiding for my life."

Vae led us toward a brick hut. "This is mine. It might be best for you to prepare here. I don't think anyone will come looking for you—"

"You cannot be serious!" Maho's voice rolled over the hillside like wind before a rainstorm. His long limbs marched over, his eyes stuck on me.

"Either aggression is a customary Tru greeting, or I am about to rip this man's spine from his body," Nkita said softly.

I stepped forward, putting myself between the males. "Maho. Perfect timing. You should meet—"

"Your mate, Emyri Izela? You...you're married to him?"

"Married is a strange word for Nkita, but if you would just calm down—"

"I want to talk with you. Alone. Now."

"We need to prepare. To leave. At once." I put a hand on Maho's chest. "Take some breaths and gather your things. There will be time to discuss relations after we see the Tonguekeeper safely back to the Queen."

"So"—Maho took big, swelling breaths, his jaw tight—"I am to stuff my feelings deep down and let them fester? I am to stop from speaking what I must speak and acting how I must act? Because you have gone and found us a mission, Izela?"

"Because the Queen of the Tru needs our help."

"Haven't you done enough for Miasi? When does it end?"

It was my turn for aggression. I shoved Maho, though it did little to move his sturdy frame. "You question my loyalty to the Queen, you question everything about me, Mahopi." I held a finger up to him. "Watch your mouth when her name is in it."

"Loyalty and stupidity are not the same thing."

"Just yesterday you considered me a traitor—"

"That's because what you did was treason. And who you did it for—"

Nkita stepped forward with a snarl. "Enough."

Rage flashed in Maho's eyes. "Yes, Crylia. Show her who you really are. Come and tear me limb from him."

Nkita reached behind him for his sword. "As you wish."

36

The Day The Battles Began

"Cryl!"

Both Nkita and Maho stepped in front of me, their broad shoulders blocking out the sun.

"Oh, it literally got dark," Vae marveled, looking up at our 'protectors'. "They're so...tall."

"That's a word for it," I grumbled. "Are you two going to stand there bumping elbows or go to arms?"

Nkita drew his sword deftly, moving toward the sound of the cry. It was Shava, no doubt on scouting duty, who saw the attackers crossing the border. She was running toward the camp with great haste, arms pumping, sword left far behind her.

Nkita took a running start and leapt atop Maho's home, standing in the wind to get a better vantage point.

"Show off," Maho said with a roll of his eyes. He ran over to meet Shava. "How many?"

"A dozen," she panted, her sienna skin ashen. "Too many."

Indeed. Too many. We were never intended to be a combat unit. Our orders were to protect the borders from stragglers, not to fend off a small battalion. But we had our Commander. And so...we all looked to Yahara, who stood with her bow and arrows.

"What do we do, Commander?" Maho asked.

Yahara stared off, thinking, unmoving. Undeciding.

"Yahara, what do we do?" Maho asked again.

But she said nothing, her lips pressed tightly together.

I took a quick breath—there wasn't time for much else—and stepped forward. "Nkita!" I called up to my mate.

He was ready. "Send the archers to the hill there, Em," he replied. "We have the advantage with the wind. They should hold until the enemy is in range. Have the tall idiot give the order."

Maho almost retaliated at Nkita, but I smacked him in the stomach before he could say a word. "Maho, take Shava and Vae. You heard him."

My friend—or rather...my former lover—kissed my forehead. "Be safe." Then he ran off, leading the other two archers.

"That leaves Beni, Yahara, and me," I called back up to Nkita.

"You and Yahara take the horses that way, east, into that tree line. Go fast, Em. Count to three hundred and then return."

"Close them in from behind?" I was already in motion toward my horse.

"Exactly. Can you manage?"

Adrenaline pulsed through my body, and energy returned. "I can."

Nkita tossed his sword down to me. I was a little surprised I caught it. But then again, we'd had time to practice before our lives fell to pieces in the Capital.

"What weapon will you use, General?"

He simply ignored me.

Of course. *He's a black wing Crylia. He is the weapon.*

"The other soldier remains with me. Up and put your back to mine. They will circle us. You call out to me, and I will swivel to attack."

"Up, Beni. With haste," I reinforced. I had to double back to drag Yahara, who was still standing frozen, feet planted on the ground.

"On your horse, Yayo. We need to ride out or we will be spotted."

She had enough sense about her to mount her steed. Then we rode off, her following behind me. Once we broke through the trees, I kept my eyes wide open, my heart pounding, my hands tight on the reins.

"I...I froze," Yahara said, her whisper breaking the silence.

"Quiet now," I warned her. "Shh."

"I am the Commander. And I *froze*."

"Yahara, you will give away our positions."

"We were under attack...and I just...froze."

I turned Beni around to face her. "And if you don't shut up, we'll die out here, run through by Cryl. Is that what you want? Close. Your. Mouth."

I had clutched the sword beneath my arm so I could maneuver Bei, but it grew heavier with each moment. The General's blade would be too large for me to wield if we were found. But I would do my best. After all, Nkita would not have sent me out here unless he knew I would be—

"Cryl be damned, that *damn Cryl*!" I shouted. I turned Bei around. "You stay right here Yayo. Stay put."

I prayed to Gua that my sister would remain frozen a bit longer as I raced back to camp, my hair flying behind me, my arm pressing the sword in place. When I arrived, I moved as quick as I could, sword drawn to slice the back of the Cryl before me.

He was not expecting my miniature ambush and he cried out as he fell to his knees, then to his face in the melting snow. I'd broken through his armor at precisely the right angle. Nkita had gone over it with me again and again. How to destroy a Crylia wearing armor.

I angled the sword like a jousting spear and urged Bei on, taking another Crylia by surprise, though this one did not fall as smoothly. He turned, wrenching the heavy sword from my grasp and pulling me off my horse.

I made myself small, ducking between his legs and yanking the sword with me so he had to either let go or fall onto his back.

When he fell, Nkita leaped from his perch atop Maho's home and landed, talons first, atop the warrior. With a gurgle, the Crylia's life faded.

Nkita growled, pulling to my feet. "You never listen!"

"You tried to trick me!" I argued as he dragged me along.

He shoved me into Maho's home and snatched the sword from me. "Give me that." Then he slammed the door shut in my face.

"Idiot," I hissed. He knew nothing about common Tru homes. The windows were glassless. I grabbed a meat carving knife from Maho's table and climbed out past the tapestry the instant he closed the door.

I ran full speed at the first Cryl I saw. Good thing, too, because he had Beni pinned to the ground, and when I rammed the blade in through the gap in his armor, just above his shoulder blades, he shook and fell over.

"Get up!" I yelled at Beni. "Get up!" I took his hand in mine and pulled him to his feet. "Where is your sword, man?"

"I don't know!" Beni had tears in your eyes. "I...l-lost it."

I took the blade from the dying Cryl and tossed it at my friend. He failed to catch it, letting it clatter to the ground.

"Beni! Take the sword and stab the killers with it! Now!"

Beni fumbled, bending and picking up his weapon.

Nkita rushed forward, knocking the gray wing off his feet, slamming him down onto the ground, and ripped both his wings from his back, leaving him bleeding and groaning beneath the black wing General's feet.

My mate grunted as he stood up. Then he faced me, casting the wings aside to the ground. "You!"

I stood, squaring off, struggling to raise the sword Beni had once again dropped. "Why is everyone...always doing that?"

"I told you to go!"

"And I didn't listen!"

"You could have gotten killed, you stupid, stupid—"

"I don't need your permission to fight for my family, *General* Nkita!" I screamed at him.

"You are not a warrior, Emyri!"

"You love to tell me what I can and cannot be, how I should and should not hold my sword. You think you own me, Nkita Opas but you are lying to yourself!"

"Then *go*! Run off and hide in your tavern and let any Cryl and any man have you. Go and be *without me* then!"

I screamed my frustration into the air and flung the sword down at Nkita's feet before marching off toward the trees. *This time, I won't be coming back.*

37

THE DAY THE SPY TURNED BACK

What am I doing? Where am I going? I stalled once I made it to the trees. My heart rate increased. My palms grew clammy. My vision blurred. *Why am I leaving? Again?*

I glanced down at my hands, shocked to find them covered in blood that was not my own. I shrieked, attempting to scrub them off on my dress. But the wool of my dress was soaked through with crimson as well.

How...many did I kill? And yes. I killed them. I took the souls from living beings, spilled their lives on the ground. When I'd fought Rizel, I couldn't bring myself to kill him. Taking the life of the King had been the most difficult feat of my young life. *So how...what possessed me to drive blades into the bodies of Cryl?*

I turned back.

Not because I felt guilty for leaving. Or because I'd made promises to my mate. But because I was frightened to be alone. And because...because I needed him.

"Em."

I blinked, startled to see him coming toward me through the trees. "I was just coming back to—"

"Are you alright?"

I tried to exhale, but my breath would not follow my orders.

Nkita wrapped strong arms around me. "Out, then in." He modeled it for me, one hand on my back, one tucking my hair behind my ear. "This is quite normal."

"Normal?" I struggled, smashing my face into his chest, my eyes closed.

"It was your first kill?"

My response was a garbled groan.

"Out, then in."

My hands finally began to shake, and I pressed them against his spine, gathering his shirt in my fists to still my quaking. "I'm afraid," I managed.

"This happens to everyone their first time."

"Not...Crylia," I gasped.

"Even Cryl, Em."

"Not you."

"Mm." He let silence cloak us for a moment. When he spoke again, he sounded distant, as though his memories echoed off the trees. "I was young."

"...H-how young?"

"Seven years."

I tensed, trying to imagine a young Nkita, his eyes wide and his steps unsteady. It was too difficult to think of him being helpless and small. "What happened?"

"You do not know how Teth are chosen, do you, Em?"

I shook my head.

"All Teth offspring are bound to the future Cza. Even if that Cza is not yet born, they are pledged. There is no choice in this matter. It is simply done. And when the old Cza is fallen and the future Cza takes the throne, those tethered to him must be selected."

"Selected?"

"We fight one another. To the death. Those who live will continue to serve as Teth, as will their offspring, and their offspring. Until the end of time."

"You...fought other Crylia? Other children?"

Nkita laughed. "Not only children. Whichever Teth had been pledged to the future Cza. Grown or not."

"You must have been so...frightened." He must have been, indeed, for my own heart still raced within me.

"There was no time for fear during combat. Those with warrior minds learn to cast aside emotion when they battle. It clouds judgment." He paused. "But afterward. When the fighting stops. And the blood no longer flows from your victims. When you find yourself filthy. And used. That is when the fear comes."

"As the water flows, all things pass."

"So says Gua?"

"Yes. So says the Goddess."

"I suppose she is not altogether ridiculous. Even if she's completely fabricated." He kissed the top of my head. Then, he growled. "What is that?"

"What...is what?"

"I can *smell him* on you."

I looked at him, my confusion replacing my alarm. "Who? The...the soldiers?"

"No. That human. He kissed you."

I sighed. "Oh, Nkita. You mean when Maho kissed my forehead? I thought you meant something serious." Then, I chuckled. "That did distract me though."

"Good. I'm glad." He moved so he could tilt my face up, so I could look into his lilac eyes. "Why don't you go find your sister. Then when you get back to camp, we can have a burial."

"For the Cryl soldiers?"

"No. For the human who touched you."

38

THE DAY THE MALES RAGED

I grabbed onto my mate's waist, digging my heels into the dirt in an effort to hold him back. "What happened to wrapping me in your arms, Nkita! I am still very fragile, remember?!"

"He needs to die." The Cryl marched forward through the trees as if my full weight were nothing but a shawl over his shoulders. "I will make it happen."

His heartbeat slowed, his progress unrelenting. "Nkita, please. Just talk to me first—"

"He put his mouth on you. I will put him in the ground."

It was then that I saw Yahara, also making her way back to camp. "Ya! A little help?"

She grimaced, her shoulders drooping. "You don't need my help to mount your Cryl, Izela."

"He is trying to kill Mahopi."

"Oh," she sighed. "Well, did you mount Mahopi, Iz?"

Nkita picked up his pace.

"Gua, no! Yahara, that is not helping!"

My sister glared at me, then raised her voice. "Monster, if you destroy our unit, we will fail at our mission. And you gave your word to our Queen and to your mate that you would help us, though I hardly understand why—"

"Yes!" I circled around, pushing Nkita's chest in an effort to stop him altogether. "You said you would help me. And if you kill my friend, I will be more useless than ever."

Nkita roared, sidestepping me and slamming his talons into a nearby tree. When he was finished assaulting nature, he turned back, his chest heaving. "Fine."

I smoothed my hair back down. "Good. Good." I faced my sister. "I am glad you are alright, Yayo—"

"He's gone."

I furrowed my brow in confusion. "I'm sorry?"

"Your Crylia." Yahara pointed to the spot where Nkita most recently stood. There was nothing left but a sad tree and the whistling wind. "He's gone."

"Oh Gua, help the helpless."

I took off as fast as I could run back to camp. Of course, Nkita was faster than I could ever hope to be. By the time I arrived, the rest of the unit was in an uproar, most of them calling for me to intervene.

Nkita had Maho cornered, the Tru-hana's back against a home. Maho held his sword, his fiery gaze set on the General. Nkita had recovered his sword as well. He stood with it at his side, his eyes locked on his opponent.

"Nkita!" I shouted. "Don't you dare!"

"He thinks he can put his *mouth on you*," my mate responded.

"You kissed Izela?" Vae cried out, her jaw dropped. "Maho, she is *wed*!"

"I didn't kiss anyone!" Maho called out. "He's out of his mind!"

I leaned my weight against Nkita, trying to steer him off course. "Nkita, it is a gesture of endearment among the Tru! Not a mating ritual! Cryl be damned, stop this!"

"I don't care what rituals and customs you claim to have." Nkita spoke so coolly that I shivered. "I know his intentions. And I do not accept them."

"*I* get to choose which intentions *I* accept. I'm my own human, General."

Yahara stepped between the rivals, using her bow to lower their swords. "This is the end of whatever nonsense you have all contrived. We are packing our things and beginning our search. Now." She breathed deep, squaring her stance. "And if anyone has a problem with that, they can stay behind. We have a Tonguekeeper to find." She looked to Nkita. "General?"

It was the first time she used his title. We all took note.

With a grunt, he nodded, sheathing his blade at his back and tucking his wing.

"And Reloa Mahopi?"

He exhaled, relaxing his sword. "Alright."

Preparations were made immediately. And once they were complete, Yahara gathered us together. "We must be smart about this as we go through Tru in search of the missing Tonguekeeper. We cannot parade this Cryl around as he is. We must disguise him. Cevae and Izela, you are responsible for accomplishing this and for teaching him enough of our customs so that he doesn't behead someone for shaking his mate's hand."

"Me?" Cevae squeaked.

"You are the most patient of the unit." Yahara mounted her horse and took the lead. "Beni and Shava, you have separate orders. I want you to go straight to the Queen. Let her know that our borders are being invaded. She should send whatever soldiers she can spare to fortify this place. Our homes are open for their use." Then, she looked at Cevae, Maho, Nkita and me. "Let's go."

Cevae spoke up. "You don't think we should split up Nkita and Maho, Commander?"

"No," Yahara said. "I don't." Then, she gave me a look. "We shall see what comes of my decision."

We readied our horses, saying goodbye to Beni and Shava, and I caught up with Yahara.

"What is it now?" she asked.

"You are meddling with my life," I whispered to her. "I know you well enough by now, I'd like to think. I see what you are trying to do."

"It's not very subtle meddling, little sister. You have gone off and let the enemy seduce you. I will give Mahopi the chance to seduce you back. It's only fair."

"It's not fair. I am wed to Nkita."

"According to his laws. Not ours. In Tru, you are free as a river koi. There is no honoring of marriage bonds made under duress. And when you are at last free of that duress, you will see clearly once more."

"Yahara, I see perfectly well."

"Those monsters have been slaughtering our family for generations, Izela. They are the reason—"

"Let me ask you a question. What do you tell Ielo to do if he sees a Crylia?"

"My son? I tell him to run."

"And if he can't run?"

"To fight."

"Should he be kind to the Crylia he is fighting?"

"These are stupid questions."

"He should show no mercy. For the sake of his own survival."

"The Crylia do not attack us because it's crucial to their survival."

I shook my head. "I have lived in their world, Yahara. If the Teth do not do exactly—and I mean *exactly*— what their Cza says, they die. And even if they do follow orders, they die. They are dedicated to him from birth, Yahara. Taught how they must think, how they must act. If the Cza wants them to find the Tonguekeeper, the

Teth will look for her. They will find her. And they will deliver her back to the Cza. Or they will face fates they will never live through."

"I know how sovereignty works, Iz. We all serve Miasi—"

"Who is gentle and kind. We worship Gua, who blesses and protects. What if you had no goddess and your queen were a tyrant? What if every day you were taught to fight her battles or face death? And look...look how things are changing for little Ielo even in this short time! How we change our ways so we can survive."

"Iz—"

"I will not be quiet. And I won't harden my heart against the Crylia like I once did. Because I have also seen, in the face of certain death, how a Cryl can choose to abandon self-preservation and help the helpless. I am not in love with Nkita Opas because I was manipulated. I am in love with him because he is the kindest living creature I have ever met. And maybe he is not as gentle as you want him to be...but he is mine. And for some reason, he has left his destiny behind to follow mine. Good luck with your scheming, Yahara. I will never change my mind."

"No," she said, calling after me as I sped up to meet the others who'd gone ahead while we spoke. "You won't change your mind, Izzy. But you'll run. You always run when it gets hard."

And, though I knew it was a wicked thing to say, I spoke. "At least I do not freeze, Yahara, and let those I love fight my battles for me." I regretted my words as soon as they left me.

Perhaps one day, my sister and I will both do better.

39

THE DAY THE GENERAL TRIED

"We are almost to the next town," Yahara said, her waist rolling as she rode Wen. "How is the disguise coming, Cevae?"

"Well, I have the cloak almost finished. It will look a bit menacing because I've included enough height to account for his wings—"

"Wing," Mahopi said.

"I'm sorry?" Cevae asked, frowning in confusion, her sweet lips bitten in with fret.

"The Cryl only has one wing," Maho clarified. "Must not be as good in battle as he lets on."

I moved my horse closer to Nkita's. "Ignore them," I said softly.

"I don't care what the humans think of me, Em." But the muscles of his forearm tensed, his jaw clenching. "I care what you think."

"Your wing is beautiful, Nkita. And I love you no less because you are missing the other."

"A Crylia female would not say such a thing. She would be ashamed—"

"She would be stupid." And then, I smirked. "Besides, I think if Mlika White Wing and I put our heads together, we'd have every female at every Vecherin drooling over you in a heartbeat. Human or Crylia, females have a thing for scars."

"It's no doubt a good thing that the two of you weren't set loose upon the unsuspecting at more Vecherins. You got Rizel removed from service after one evening, if I remember correctly." He growled. "And I will have him removed from life if still he's in possession of his."

I grinned. "What do you think was so valuable that Letti would have traded me for it?"

"Well, it couldn't have been that important if Rizel parted with it so quickly, just to get his hands on some frustrating little Tru girl with a perfect arse—"

I reached over to smack him, but he caught my hand and brought it to his lips.

I blushed like a child and had to clear my throat. "Now, when we get to Kiepo, you need to bring out your inner spy."

"I am not unfamiliar with espionage, Em."

"I know. But...I am more Tru than you will ever be. You helped me in Crylia. I will help you here, if you'll let me. I will teach you."

He nodded his head. "Go on."

"You need to move more slowly. But also think less before you do."

"How can those two directives coincide?"

"We Tru are very instinctual. We flow. Like water. If you reach for something, do it without calculation. Cryl are always overthinking. We don't do that."

"So think more about not overthinking?"

"Exactly."

He sighed. "Is that all?"

"You will have to walk like you are not so powerful."

"What...do you mean? I walk normally."

I snorted. And apparently Cevae was listening as well because she snorted too. "Oh, General. No. You walk like you have just slain a thousand unkillable beasts and are unafraid to face the ten thousand ahead."

"That's how walking works."

"Not if you're pretending to be Tru."

Yahara stopped us, leaving our horses to graze in the open pastures outside of Kiepo. "Practice," she told Nkita. "Or we'll be found out in an instant."

"We should just leave him here," Maho grumbled. "Why do we even need him while we look for the Tonguekeeper in Kiepo?"

"He is the only one of us who actually knows what to look for," Yahara countered. "Apparently, Cryl are well aware that this builder of worlds exists."

Maho scoffed. "*Gua* builds worlds."

"If Gua didn't want the Tonguekeeper to exist, she wouldn't, Maho," I explained. "Queen Miasi says this is important for the survival of both our worlds. Nkita is on our side here." I nodded at my mate. "Why don't you try walking like a Tru."

Nkita stepped through the pasture, his boots crushing the green grass that had poked up through the patches of snow.

"Oh, he looks so *scary*," Vae said, her eyes wide. "That's no good." She waved at Maho. "Show him how to look harmless when you walk, Maho. No one is afraid of you."

"I am *very* intimidating," Maho snapped.

We all chuckled, even Yahara.

"Drop your shoulders, Nkita," I told him. "And let your hips swing a little more. Step like you're minding the grass."

"Why would I mind *grass*?"

"Because you wouldn't want to crush everything in your path!" Vae said, grinning. "Be gentle!"

"To grass?"

"To *everything*!"

He groaned. "No wonder you can't fight. You are all concerned with...with whether you'll scrape a bit of bark or crush the snow—"

"Ahhh!" Yahara said, trying to startle Nkita.

He stood still as stone, save for the raising of one eyebrow. "What was that?"

Yahara threw her hands in the air. "You need natural human reflexes, Cryl!"

Nkita wrinkled his nose. "Like a *coward*?"

I held my hands up, anticipating the cries of outrage from the group. "Nkita, give us a startle, if you don't mind."

He shrugged. "Alright. Try again, Commander."

Yahara jumped out at him, and Nkita stepped backward, his facial expression unchanging, and gasped. "Ah."

"He's so bad at this," Vae marveled. "Look sad, Nkita!"

"Sad?"

"Mhmm."

"I'm never sad."

Vae giggled. "Then look happy."

He gave exactly half of one smirk.

Vae applauded that one. "Alright, if you don't mind, try looking...lost in love."

"Lost in it?"

"Yes!"

"Why would I be lost in love? I see the love. I strategize toward the love. I attack the love. I devour—"

"Alright, that's enough." I looked to Yahara. "What is our strategy for entering the town?"

"We will pitch in around Kiepo, as guests often do when visiting new towns. Get to talking. Find out if the Tonguekeeper has been spotted. Maho, you can join the fishermen. Vae, the netmenders. Iz, the casters. I will find the herders. And Nkita, you make your rounds and visit each of us in case we've found a lead."

"It's a good strategy," Nkita said. "We are looking for someone who is able to change fate. There may be some suspicions about them."

"What does that even mean?" Maho asked.

"They can lift something too heavy for them," I chimed in, "or move unmovable things. Odd behavior, strange speech."

"You speak like you've seen her," Yahara said, narrowing her eyes.

"I can't be sure. But I know we will find her."

As we walked to the town, Nkita slid his hand over my lower back, pulling me into a quick embrace. "You were a caster?" he asked. "What is that?"

I sighed, letting his touch relax my body. "A caster throws out nets to harvest fish."

"Doesn't the dead man do that?"

"No, Maho is a diver. It's very different. Also please do not kill Maho."

"Fish are fish."

221

"You are in for a surprising day, General. And...I performed many tasks among my people. Not only the world of a caster."

"Oh?"

"Mm. I was a storyteller."

"That is an entire occupation here?"

I studied him for a moment. The sharp lines of his face, glowing in the Tru sunshine. It was like finding a snow leopard asleep in a bed of flowers. "Yes. I went to people as they worked, as they cooked, as they reveled and danced, as they died, as they gave birth. And I told the stories of our people."

"Is that what you did for the Queen?"

"Miasi and I have known each other a long time. I...worked for her father. But that is a story this teller does not like revisiting." My stomach soured as I forced the memories of the King to leave my mind.

"Another time," Nkita said, his hand applying steady pressure to my spine. "I have my lost stories as well. I understand."

What stories does this Cryl keep from me? For I knew that even if he did not show it, sadness and pain and loss had ravaged him more than most. I felt it when he touched me, when his lips met mine, when he moved inside me. The depth of the life he'd lived, the ghosts of the deaths he'd evaded.

"Are you nervous about working among my people?" I asked him.

"I am...tentative."

"I will help you. Like you helped me."

He kissed my forehead. Then kissed it again.

"Alright, Grand Teth. Now you own my forehead. Does that please you?"

"A little." He sighed. "But I'll kill him one day anyway. I just have to be...patient."

40

THE DAY THE NETS WERE CAST

I loved the way the river rolled past my calves on its way. The rough cords of the nets scratched against my fingers, for it had been too long since I was able to fish, but I looked forward to the blisters. I missed even the most terrible parts of being Tru.

The women laughed when a younger girl slipped, the net catching her toes when she cast it. She was new to the river but she would learn. One of her aunts—or maybe a sister or cousin—pulled her up and tugged on her braid with a chuckle.

The girl blushed, clearly embarrassed, and tried her cast again. This time, the net spread wide, and a woman at the other end of the flowing river caught it with ease.

"You are new to Kiepo?" someone asked me, elbowing me with a sweet smile. "Welcome. The water suits you."

"Thank you," I replied. "The rivers are yours. I am just passing through, I'm afraid."

"Come to our home for dinner, then! We have room for one more. Unless you have company with you. Then we have room for as many as you need." She laughed at her own joke.

"I will see if we are able."

"You cast nets well," said another, her golden hair so long that it hung into the water at her waist. "But you move like a weaver too."

"That's because she is no caster and no weaver," an old Tru grunted. The woman was a fish chaser, despite her old age. She would shoo the fish into our nets as they came, stepping gracefully along the river rocks without missing a step. No doubt, she had been doing it her whole life. Most likely she learned it from her grandmother.

"She isn't?" the girl asked.

I'm not? I tried to stay calm. *Do they know me as a traitor? Will they turn on me once they find me out?*

"She is a storyteller," the old woman finished. "And from the look of her, a damn good one."

"A storyteller!" the women gasped. "We have not had one in Kiepo for ages."

"How can you tell?" I asked the elder.

She paused her work, frowning at me, her wrinkles deeply grooved into her beautiful face. "You are quiet, first of all. Listening. People think storytellers do a lot of talking. But the good ones...they listen more than they speak. That's how they find the best stories."

"By listening to our gossip?" one of the women gasped.

"No, foolish child. By listening to what Gua is saying. Beneath the noise you make with your chattering. Beneath the current rushing past us. The whispers of the goddess, revealing the stories."

The girl's eyes widened. "You hear Gua? Whispering?"

I smiled, my entire body tingling in anticipation as I began. "The wild wolf crosses the chasm and stands at the edge of a cliff."

They squealed, leaving their nets, eyes wide. "She's *starting*," they whispered.

I went on. "The wild wolf only has two choices. He can either make his home on the edge of the cliff...or go back the way he came. What does the wild wolf do?"

One woman spoke up. "I would go back if I were the wolf."

Another pondered. "Wait...why did the wolf go to the cliff? Why did he leave the forest in the first place?"

"The wild wolf once lived with his pack among the trees. But fires came, with flames that towered beyond the clouds. The fires separated him from his pack and pushed him to the very edge of the highest cliff."

"Oh, then I would make my home on the edge of the cliff," another said.

"And there your story would end. But that is not what the wild wolf chooses. For he remembers that always there is another choice. The wild wolf lifts his voice to Gua. He howls and mourns for those he lost. He howls and begs for the future he cannot reach. He howls and prays that the goddess would come."

"And Gua sent the rain?"

"No."

"But...but Gua helps the helpless."

"The wild wolf finishes his prayers. Then, he gathers his courage and...leaps from the cliff."

The women gasped, jaws dropped.

"The wild wolf lands in the river below, safe from the flames and safe from the fall. Gua helps the helpless. But she *loves* the courageous. So ask yourself this, you casters of nets, when the flames come next and the cliff is all you have. Is it Gua's help you want most? Or her *love*?"

The woman applauded, their faces drawn in wonder.

"Back to work," said the old woman. "All the fish have passed us by. We must work twice as hard now." Then, she came to me. "You are indeed a good storyteller, girl."

"Thank you, elder."

"What payment do you want? They don't know they ought to pay you for your gift."

"I am looking for someone, actually. Perhaps you have seen her?"

"Describe the one you seek."

"She takes words and makes wonders. Someone odd in that way."

The woman sucked air in through her teeth. "What do you want with such a being?"

"I will give my life to protect her."

The woman smiled a toothless grin. "There is the courage, I see." She motioned for me to follow her. "I have found someone who matches that description. Come. I will take you to her."

I followed the woman as she hobbled along the river bank, headed to a grove of trees. "What is your name?" I asked her.

"Kashila," she replied. "I'm too old to remember the rest of the name, so Kashila will do." She batted a willow branch out of the way. "And you will not tell me yours, I imagine."

"Because I am a mysterious storyteller?"

"Because you are the one who killed the King."

I froze, my heart arrested.

"Keep up. I could drop dead at any moment, and then you will not find your stranger. Never keep the elderly waiting."

And so I followed her until we came upon the strangest sight. A young Tru-ori girl, trapped in a net, tied to a rock.

"What...what is this?!"

"This young thing followed you here. Saw her the moment she arrived. Thought it was odd, someone trailing a storyteller like that. I figured maybe she meant to rob you. Or turn you in for a reward."

"Why would you seek to help me like that, Kashila?"

"Because"—and she reached out and smacked my chest—"Gua loves you, girl. And I love Gua. So...I will help you not die before your time. It's important."

"Thank you so much for your kindness...but who is this girl? I think she must have been following me for some time—"

"Every time I talk to her, she steals my breath right out of my lungs. I leave her to you, Storyteller. Gua bless your efforts."

I swallowed, alone with the girl in the net. "H-hello, Tonguekeeper."

41

THE DAY THE ONE RAN FREE

"I mean you no harm—"

"Sep roihm."

When she said the words, my very bones turned on one another, as if I was being folded like a wool blanket. I hurried backward, stumbling as I tried to escape the pain.

The girl did not look like she wished to hurt me. Her blue eyes were wide, her body trembling. She seemed more frightened than vengeful.

Strange indeed to hear a Tru speak Old Cryl. I held my hand up to her. "I will keep my distance. And go get an interpreter. Please. Do not worry. I will help you as best I can. You have my word."

I turned on my heel, headed back to the river. Sloshing into the water, I whispered into Kashila's ear, asking her to make sure nothing hurt the girl until I could return.

Then, I raced back to the town in search of my mate.

"Iz!" Maho called, spotting me from the harbor. "Iz, over here!"

I ran up to him, trying to catch my breath. "Maho—"

"Your lover almost drowned our entire crew today. I hope you know he is absolutely mad. Who takes a sword onto a sea-bound vessel?! And he weighs enough that the entire thing—"

"I found her."

"—took on water. So half the crew had to bail us out while we—"

"Maho, I found her."

"—I have never been more embarrassed in my life. And Vae said he ripped more holes in the nets than he mended—"

"Mahopi, for the love of Gua, let your words rest for once!"

He frowned. "Well, that wasn't very nice—"

"*I found her.*"

"You...you did? Already? So...so quickly? I thought this would take months!"

"I need Nkita. She speaks Old Cryl."

"What? How? And...why would she speak—?"

"*Nkita.* Where is he?"

"Helping Yahara. And by helping, I mean destroying the livelihoods of many, no doubt. He has probably eaten all the sheep or something—"

"Find Vae. I'll go to the pastures. Meet me at the river where the casters throw their nets."

The pastures were a good distance away, and I found that my injuries made me crave more herbs. But that would have to come later. I was prepared to ask if any herders had seen an irrevocably frightening human with lilac eyes, but...it was easy enough to spot my mate.

He stood on a boulder, about a hundred sheep bleating around him and herders gathered, all muttering and pointing at him.

"Yahara?" I asked, finding my sister among the herders. "What...is—?"

"They all *love* him," she said, clearly annoyed. "Can you believe it?"

"The...the sheep? What am I looking at here?"

"The *herders* love him too. They said they served the Queen's Army and that Nkita saved them. The Good General, they called him. And I cannot get any of them to leave the Cryl alone."

So much for hiding that Nkita was Crylia.

"Em!" he called to me. "Emyri, *help me*."

"Why are you up there, General?"

"The sheep. They will not stop."

"You are a mighty monster. Part bird of prey, part lion, part serpent. And you fear *sheep*?"

"Their affection is both aggressive and unreciprocated, Em. Distract them."

"Just come down."

"They will bleat all over me!"

232

I laughed and opened my arms. "Jump, mighty Cryl. I will catch you."

He glared at me. "You will drop me like a stone."

"Well, we found what we are looking for. Come down with haste. I need you."

Nkita leaped over the sheeps' heads and bounded away from the pasture, cloak billowing behind him. Yahara and I followed, both grinning from ear to ear.

I caught up to Nkita, we found Maho and Vae, and all of us made it back to the river.

"Thank you, Kashila," I said, kissing the old woman's hands.

"I will go make you dinner now." She scowled at us. "All five of you, I suppose. Six if you count the strange one in the net." Then, the old woman sauntered off toward the town.

"You put the Tonguekeeper in a net?" Yahara said. "Iz, what were you thinking?" She rushed forward before I could stop her.

"*Sep roihm.*"

Yahara screamed, stumbling backward to escape the pain.

"She does that," I explained. "I don't know what she's saying, but none of us can get her out of the net unless we figure out—"

"I am harm," Nkita translated. "That's what it means in Old Cryl."

"She...*is* harm?"

"That's what she's saying. I don't know how she could be making those words a reality without being the Tonguekeeper. Is this who you met before, Em?"

I shook my head. "She looks nothing like Letti. This girl is Tru, first of all. Letti was a gray wing Crylia. But I think she has been...following me?"

Nkita growled. "For how long?"

"Since I met Letti outside of Yogdn."

"I would have noticed," Nkita said.

"I would have too," Maho added.

"This isn't a competition," I said. "It doesn't matter if either of you noticed. *I* noticed. And so did that elder or she wouldn't have caught her in this net. Now...how do we get her back to the Queen if we can't get near her—"

"We convince her that we mean her no harm?" Vae said.

But Nkita took a breath. "*Sep krov vanya crystin. Sep yo.*"

The girl squirmed and let out that same breath. "*Sep roihm. Sep yo.*"

"Let us come," Nkita said. "We only want to help you all."

You all? I tried to understand, but my thoughts were muddled. *What is Nkita talking about? What can he mean?*

"She told me I cannot get close." The girl shook her head, trying to scurry away. "Only distance."

"Why were you following Emyri?"

"We like her."

234

"What do you want with Emyri?"

"Want?"

"Why follow her *here*?"

"Because. We like her." The girl tilted her head. "She is our courage."

Vae gasped. "That's what I always say!"

"Help me," the girl said, her eyes tearing. "Help me. I am too tired to keep running."

"We cannot get near you."

"Then how will I get out? H-how will I escape her when she comes?"

"We can throw you a knife so you can sever and split the rope. Can you catch it?"

The girl nodded. Nkita tossed her a sheathed dagger, and we all waited while she slit the knots of the net. When she was free, she scrambled to her feet and took off through the woods.

"After her!" Yahara shouted. "We cannot keep her safe if we lose her."

42

THE DAY THE VESSEL WEPT

Nkita was fastest. And when we all split up to find the girl, I followed after him. Suddenly, he stopped, pulling me back behind a tree.

I kept silent, peering out from between the branches. Up ahead, the girl had stopped cold. She appeared to be more frightened than ever, still as ice. *Perhaps...listening?*

"Who is coming for her? Why is she so afraid? Is it the Hresh?"

"There," Nkita whispered, pointedly ignoring me. "Someone is chasing her."

"How did you know what to say to her? Nkita...tell me the truth of what is happening—"

"We move. Now."

"Wait! I have questions—"

Nkita raced forward, sword drawn. But he did not get to the Tonguekeeper before Letti did.

The girl screamed as Letti shrieked a string of Old Cryl and plunged a twisted blade into her throat.

Discarding the body of the girl, Letti faced us, her breathing ragged, her face drenched in perspiration and her hands shaking. "*Sep cliva. Sep roihm.*"

Nkita fell to his knees, his body writhing in agony. "*Sep cliva. Sep roihm. Sep krov vanya crystin—*"

Nkita cried out, his talons piercing the half-frozen ground as Letti gripped the blade, her eyes locked on him. *She will kill him. She will kill him right in front of me, here in this forest.* I felt his pain surge through my own body, twisting my bones, curling my blood. I raced forward with everything I had in me. *Gua. Help.* It was my turn to show courage, yet again. "Letti! *Stop!*"

She did stop when she saw me, panting, her wild eyes focusing. "*Oahra?*"

"What...have you done, Letti?"

"I"—her hands shook so violently that I was sure she would drop the blade she gripped. "Stay away." But her voice was weak. A whisper.

"You...killed the Tonguekeeper—"

"The Tonguekeeper?" Letti gave a raspy laugh, and quiet tears spilled down her cheeks. "Her? No. No." She shook her head as a sob left her. "But I did kill her, didn't I?" She glanced at the dagger. "And...I should have killed him when I had the chance."

"Letti...why? Kill...kill Nkita...why?"

"Umra," she corrected. "My name...is Umra. I wish I could have been Letti. But instead, she is dead. My friend is...dead at my feet." She pointed at Nkita, who she still held in pain on the ground. "I have to stop the Cza." Then, she stared at me. "And you. I should have, back in Led. But...." She sobbed. "I am so tired. I am so, so tired now."

She came for me. Umra took the last of her strength and ran forward. I dodged her, slipping in a patch of ice. She was on me again in a moment, the red and violet blade humming as it drew nearer and nearer to me. I struggled to keep her away, to keep her from slipping the blade into my throat. My bones began to splinter, my skin threatening to shred itself in her presence.

"*Sep cliva,*" she gasped.

I screamed, my mind beginning to empty itself against my will.

"*Sep roihm....*"

Pain came in fresh waves, like lightning in my body. But still, I struggled against the blade.

"*Sep—*"

Gua. Please. And with one last try, I swiveled, taking Umra down to the ground beneath me. To my great shock, Umra, the tavernkeeper's mate, plunged the twisted blade into her own throat, her eyes bulging.

Nkita groaned, dragging himself to his feet. He grabbed me, dragging me away from Umra's twitching body.

"What...what just happened—?" I asked, my mind and body numb.

"I must get that blade, Em. We have to run—"

"Tell me what happened!" I screamed, pounding my fists on the forest floor. "Tell me the truth!"

"The...three—"

"*Nkita Opas!*"

"I don't know, Emyri!"

"Just tell me. If you want me to survive the truth of what I have just done—"

"It's not your fault—"

"I killed the Tonguekeeper, Nkita!" Somehow. I remembered how Umra feared me on that mountain top in Led. As if she'd truly realized who I was for the first time.

Nkita drew a deep breath. "The truth is complicated."

"I will decide what is beyond my comprehension. Tell. Me."

"The Tonguekeeper teaches three to be her replacement. Blesses them and speaks words over them none can hear. She calls to them from the moment of their birth, it's said. And she guides them to her. One holds her harm. One holds her cunning. One holds her courage. In the end, one is chosen."

"The girl...Letti. She was the Tonguekeeper's harm."

"I believe so."

"And Umra? Her cunning?"

"Perhaps. Yes."

"Why? Why would Umra...?"

"Only the twisted blade can kill a Tonguekeeper or her Vessels, Emyri."

"That is what Umra took from Rizel?" I shook my head. "Why kill her...her partner? Why would one Vessel kill another?"

"I...don't know."

"Why did she know you...why did she call you the Cza?"

"I'm not certain."

I nodded, knowing my mate was lying to me. Knowing there was more he refused to tell. "We have to get rid of that blade. If it falls into the wrong hands, the third vessel and the true Tonguekeeper—"

"Em, you're not understanding."

"Nkita. You have to accept what the rebels are doing on your behalf. It's the only way to keep us all safe. To put power and strength behind Miasi's efforts. You must accept that you are to be the Cza of Crylia."

"I cannot do that, Em. I will never do that."

"I will convince you."

"You may try and you will most certainly fail. My blade will only serve one, so long as I live. But right now, we need to get you out of these woods. Out of Kiepo. Out of Tru."

Nkita rushed to the dagger, lifted it with care, and placed it beneath his cloak.

"We must meet up with Yahara," I told him.

"No," he said. "We must return to Miasi without delay."

"We can't just—"

But Nkita was already moving. We made it back to the horses and rode hard to the Home of the Queen, my sister and the rest of our unit left far behind us.

"Move," Nkita said, shoving past the guards until we made it all the way to the Queen's Hall.

Miasi was holding a meeting of sorts, and she dismissed those gathered upon sight of us. She stood, her white and gold gown floating around her. "General. Izela—"

"The Vessels are dead," Nkita said.

Miasi held her composure, but her face lost its color. "All three Vessels are gone?"

"Two are dead. I found the third."

Miasi and Nkita stared at one another for quite some time. Then, Miasi nodded. "What must we do to protect her now?"

I interrupted. "Who is this vessel? And why was I not told that these vessels exist? Why was I not told...anything?"

Miasi struggled to speak through the emotion she held back. "We will protect you, Emyri Izela. Even if I must trade all of Tru to do it."

I blinked. "I...would never hear of such a thing. Miasi, you are my *Queen*."

But Miasi lowered her head to me. "Only one Vessel remains. We cannot—"

"What does it *mean*?"

"You, Em." Nkita said it, the words falling from his mouth and nearly slicing my soul to pieces.

I stumbled away from him, laughing. "What are you talking about, Nkita?"

"Em. I am sorry...."

No.

I marched through the corridors and found my way into a spare room. I closed the door behind me, with every intention of finding a way out of the window.

But Nkita was on my heels.

He caught me by the waist, turning me to face him. "Slow down," he told me.

"I am not...*anything*," I told him. I shoved him, pushing him away from me. "Do not try to make me into something now."

"This is not my doing, Emyri, and you know it."

"I am just a Tru! Just a human. Just a spy. Just a traitor. I can barely wrap my mind around being your *mate*. Now there is some...some destiny—?"

"You know who she is." Nkita spoke with certainty. "You know."

I crumpled to the ground. I knew. I could see her face smiling at me. The way she comforted me with the sign of the Tru as I hid her among the roots of a tree. *Drosya. Drosya the Grounded.*

"I...have to find her, Nkita," I wept.

"We will."

"I should never have left her behind..."

"I was too stubborn to listen. Too blind to understand."

I shook my head, touching his strong chest. "I am not the important one of the two of us, Grand Teth. The rebels are waiting for you to take your place. For you to challenge the Cza of Crylia—"

"I cannot be Cza if I am to keep you safe. It will require all my devotion. All my attention. Protecting you, Em, will forever be the most important occupation in the history of Miror. Knowing you will be my legacy."

"Nkita. I won't accept this. It's not possible. I cannot even speak Old Cryl."

"I will teach you."

"I cannot even make it through one Vecherin without—"

"I will teach you."

"I cannot face the Cza. Or the Hresh. Or—"

"I will teach you."

Tears abandoned their orders, spilling down my face. "I just want to...to slow this down. And to not be fragile. And to not be courageous. And to not be anyone's Vessel, or anyone's spy, or anyone's sister or champion. I don't want to be anyone's only hope. I just want to be—"

"Name it."

"I want to be clean and warm. And I want to be the only thing you think about. I want to have you touch me exactly right and for exactly as long as I desire. No interruptions. And I want you to be whole. And happy. And full. I want to trade my courage for your happiness. I want to trade my rivers for your storms. But I don't know how to have any of that now. I don't know how to make any of that real. I don't want this madness. I want a *future*, Nkita. With *you*."

Nkita One Wing, Grand Teth to the Cza, First General of the Crylia Army, mate to the last Vessel of Miror, put his hand around my throat and waited for me to put my hand around his.

"I will teach you," he said, "as long as you promise to teach me. We will find her, Em."

Slowly, still weeping, I put my palm against the slow pulse of my mate, curling my fingers around his neck. I would let him kiss me, I knew. And I would open myself to him. Let his hands rip my clothes off my body. Let his tongue draw circles on my skin.

And then, when he was deep in sleep...I would gather all the courage I had left...and I would run. I would run and never, ever let myself be found again.

THE END

More

By Teshelle Combs

Scan to read the
The First Collection
And other books.

Review
This Book

Scan to leave
a review for

RIVERS FOR STORMS

The First
Collection

The First Dryad 1 & 2

A forbidden love, slow-burn, magically-enchanted romance

The First Stone

An enemies to lovers, arranged marriage, romantic adventure

The First Nymph

A haunting enemies to lovers, star-crossed, fantasy romance

The First Flame

A forbidden love, romantic action, royal drama

The First Breath

A fast burn, forbidden love, mystical, heartbreaking romance

The First Muse

A sweeping, age gap, classical romance

The First Dragon

A chaos-fueled, fated mates romance

The First Spark

Coming soon

The First Shadow

Coming soon

The First Collection
Reading Paths

The First Collection is a series of standalone novels woven together to create a cohesive fantasy romance experience. Choose your own path to piece together the puzzle, or select one of these 10 paths to curate a journey for your personality!

The Romantic

You are bound to love. Read it all in the most romantic flow, ending with a happily ever after.

1. The First Dryad 1
2. The First Muse
3. The First Nymph
4. The First Flame
5. The First Breath
6. The First Dragon
7. The First Stone
8. The First Dryad 2

The Warrior

You are fearless. Attack the most soul-shattering stories first.

1. The First Breath
2. The First Nymph
3. The First Muse
4. The First Dryad 1
5. The First Dryad 2
6. The First Flame
7. The First Dragon
8. The First Stone

The Adventurer

You crave a good epic tale. Read it all as one adventurous thrill.

1. The First Muse
2. The First Stone
3. The First Nymph
4. The First Flame
5. The First Breath
6. The First Dryad 1
7. The First Dryad 2
8. The First Dragon

The Purist

You don't mess with perfection. Read in the exact order the books were written.

1. The First Dryad 1
2. The First Stone
3. The First Nymph
4. The First Flame
5. The First Dryad 2
6. The First Breath
7. The First Muse
8. The First Dragon

The Elementalist

You are one with nature.
Read with each element
grouped together.

1. The First Flame
2. The First Dragon
3. The First Dryad 1
4. The First Dryad 2
5. The First Breath
6. The First Muse
7. The First Nymph
8. The First Stone

The Scholar

You crave information.
Read in the order that fills
in the most details first.

1. The First Dragon
2. The First Dryad 1
3. The First Dryad 2
4. The First Nymph
5. The First Breath
6. The First Stone
7. The First Muse
8. The First Flame

The Heartcrusher

You aren't afraid to cry.
Read from happiest to
most devastating.

1. The First Stone
2. The First Dragon
3. The First Flame
4. The First Dryad 1
5. The First Dryad 2
6. The First Muse
7. The First Nymph
8. The First Breath

The Historian

You are a defender of order.
Read along with the true
timeline of the overall story.

1. The First Breath
2. The First Stone
3. The First Flame
4. The First Dragon
5. The First Dryad 1
6. The First Dryad 2
7. The First Nymph
8. The First Muse

The Chaos

You like to tempt fate and tease
your brain. Read in the most
unnatural order possible.

1. The First Dragon
2. The First Muse
3. The First Nymph
4. The First Stone
5. The First Dryad 2
6. The First Flame
7. The First Breath
8. The First Dryad 1

The Maverick

You don't color inside the lines.
Choose your own journey in any
order you wish!

Books
Kindle and Paperback

The Underglow

I confessed to myself that I had paid very little attention to the countless governesses who attempted to explain the general rules of romantic engagement for Femmes of my stature and upbringing. But despite my lack of knowledge of general rules, I had a general sense that I was breaking them, whatever they were. Generally speaking, of course.

Closer should have made me nervous. I was not nervous, however, and so closer I went until there was no separation between his hips and mine. This was a relief to me—one difficult to explain. For I did not think there could ever be such closeness between another living thing and myself. Truly, I did not think, though they claimed to desire it, that any other living thing wanted to be so close to me.

<<You withhold>>, Alexander meant to me, pulling my bottom lip between his before pressing his mouth fully to mine. I felt only the slightest prick of his fangs, for he had not lengthened them. With my head nearly swimming, I wondered if he would sink those fangs into me as he once did. But no. Instead, he intended. <<I will be patient>>.

I detested patience. It was a monster that society told its victims was required, but really, it only convinced us all to work longer hours while they fattened us up for the slaughter. What is the point of patience? Who does it serve but the impatient ones?

I wrapped my arms around his waist and held firmly, but he released my grip rather easily.

<<Patience>>. With a last touch of his thumb to my lip and a final probe of his considerate eyes, he stepped away. <<I will find who hurt you>>.

I truthfully thought he had forgotten about this, as it had left my mind entirely. The idea that he would seek some vengeance on my behalf made my hands go numb, for it led me to envision Alexander strung up in a dark dungeon, awaiting Sleep. Surely he would be captured. Surely he would be enslaved once more. Surely I would not be able to save him. Chivalry was not something I required from this pyre.

But he looked at me—some small distance between us—in such a way that I could not believe it was chivalry compelling him.

<<You do not wish me to find them>>, he meant. The feeling of his meaning came slow and hot, like waves against a stone on too warm of a day. Or like standing too close to a flame. This is what it felt like for Alexander to be cross with me.

I wondered if I should be worried that I enjoyed the feeling.

And then I felt a shift in him, or rather, felt it come from him. <<I will go>>.

Books
Kindle and Paperback

Slit Throat Saga

"My people," he said, yelling over the toning, "let's celebrate. For today, the one who breaks the laws of nature, the one who moves the unmovable, the one who tests the very hands of God, will be set back on the right path. The Fight is not in vain."

He turned with a flourish to watch with us all as a translucent synthetix blade, held tight in the Moral's fist, sliced across the throat of the girl. A gurgle, then her blonde head flopped forward. Her blood gushed brilliant red. One would think it meant that the Fight was mistaken, that she was just like everyone else—a normal human with no unearthly capabilities, no deadly tendencies. Her blood seemed pure and red, filled with iron just like it should be. But after a few seconds, as her strength faded, the red diluted and her blood ran clear as a mountain river.

She was Meta. Just like they thought and I'm sure as they determined when she was confined in the House of Certainty for questioning. No true metal in her veins. No metal in her whole body. Not even metal in her mind. Instead she could pull it to her. She was a magnet. An abomination. And if left uncaught and unkilled, her kind would destroy the world.

The people—my people—cheered along with the Best Of Us as the Meta's watery blood poured over her small breasts, down her loose linen shirt, over the wooden platform, and through the street. It always amazed me how long Meta could bleed, how much life they held in their bodies. We all waited until the flow pooled beneath our feet, Ender Stream blessing us with one final reminder: *If you are us, you live, and if you are them, you die.*

"Well, Nex," Onur said with a little sigh as the crowd began to disperse, shoes squelching in the remains of the Meta girl, "what must be done is done." He brushed my thick, silver curls behind my ear so he could kiss my temple again, his favorite habit. His pale skin seemed to shine against my dusty red complexion. He looked tired, but he smiled. "We should get something to eat, yes?"

I smiled back at him, turning and tiptoeing so I could reach his lips with my own. His were soft and yielding, warm and inviting. Mine were not quite as full, not quite as tender. I met his eyes, ensuring that my gaze said exactly what I needed it to. *All Fight, no fear.* "Yes, let's eat. We can say cheers to the next one to be found."

I stepped through the Stream, one hand tight in my love's. The other hand I kept stuffed in the pocket of my cotton dress, clenched, but not so firmly that my fingernails might draw blood from my palm. That would not do. For the Stream soaking through my shoes was no less damned than the blood coursing through my veins.

Careful, Nex.

Careful.

Books

Kindle and Paperback

Tuck Me In

I stepped toward him. "Marrow, you walked from There to Here? That must have taken hours. You could have been hurt. You could have been killed."

He nodded. "I did not know that when I set out, but I am aware of the dangers now. There were many."

"So you're not alright. Oh Dios." I rubbed my chest. My heart was definitely not stopped anymore. It raced, banging against its cage. "I might actually be sick."

"Bel...."

I smacked my hands together. "Marrow, what were you thinking?"

He didn't answer. But I found the sadness growing in his dark eyes.

"I'm sorry I'm yelling," I said. And I was so sorry. He didn't know why I was so upset, why the thought of him coming all this way was nightmare-inducing rather than a wonderful surprise.

That's when, without being able to stop myself, I reached out and touched his elbow.

Now, I knew—I knew—I was not supposed to touch my subject. It was on every Grade test I had ever taken. We can't study something if we manipulate it. If we handle it. If we hold it.

But my hand on his elbow led to him leaning into me. He wrapped both arms around me and put his cheek to my hair. And he lingered. In his still, slow way.

I clutched the back of his shirt and pressed my face to his chest and fought the tears that came to my eyes.

"You're okay," he said calmly, with that voice that sounded like magic being born. Like a fantasy opening its eyes.

That was the first time I realized how much everything hurt, all the time, from every direction, and how much I wished it would all stop.

Everything, that is, except for a Glimpse named Marrow.

Books

Kindle and Paperback

CORE SERIES

Ava is the kind of girl who knows what's real and what isn't. Nothing in life is fair. Nothing is given freely. Nothing is painless. Every foster kid can attest to those truths, and Ava lives them every day. But when she meets a family of dragon shifters and is chosen to join them as a rider, her very notion of reality is shaken. She doesn't believe she can let her guard down. She doesn't think she can let them in—especially not the reckless, kind-eyed Cale. To say yes to him means he would be hers—her dragon and her companion—for life. But what if Ava has no life left to give?

The System Series

1 + 1 = Dead. That's the only math that adds up when you're in the System. Everywhere Nick turns, he's surrounded by the inevitability of his own demise at the hands of the people who stole his life from him. That is, until those hands deliver the bleeding, feisty, eye-rolling Nessa Parker. Tasked with keeping his new partner alive, Nick must face all the ways he's died and all the things he's forgotten.

Nessa might as well give up. The moment she gets into that car, the moment she lays her hazel eyes on her new partner, her end begins. It doesn't matter that Nick Masters can slip through time by computing mathematical algorithms in his mind. It doesn't matter how dark and handsome and irresistibly cold he is. Nessa has to defeat her own shadows. Together and alone, Nick and Nessa make sense of their senseless fates and fight for the courage to change it all. Even if it means the System wins and they end up...

well...dead.

Poetry
Thoughts Like Words

Let There Be Nine Series

- *Let There Be Nine Vol 1*: **Enneagram Poetry**
- *Let There Be Nine Vol 2*: **Enneagram Poetry**

For Series: Words laced together on behalf of an idea, a place, a world.

- **For Her**
- **For Him**
- **For Them**
- **For Us**

Love Bad Series: Poems About Love. Not Love Poems.

- **Love Bad**
- **Love Bad More**
- **Love Bad Best**

Standalone Poetry Books:

BREATH LIKE GLASS

Poems for love that never lasts.

Girl Poet

A collection of poems on the passion, privilege, and pain of being (or not quite being) a girl.

FRAMELESS

A collection of poems for the colors that make life vibrant, from their perspective, so we may share in what they might think and feel.

This One Has Pockets

Narrative poetry about a girl who is near giving up and the boy who tries to save her.

ON THE NATURE OF HINGES

A series of poetic questions from the perspective of someone who has been left behind more than once.

Gray Child

A unique expression of being more than one race, written by a Caribbean American woman, for anyone who cares to read.

Contact Teshelle Combs

Instagram | @TeshelleCombs

Facebook | TC's Fantasy and Dystopian Readers

Leave A Review

A good review is how you breathe life into my story. Please leave RIVERS FOR STORMS an Amazon review and tell a friend how much you love Em and Nkita.